Not Just Cricket...

First published in India in 2010 by CinnamonTeal Publishing

Copyright © 2010 Vikram Dravid
ISBN: 978-93-80151-56-4

Cover Images: Author, Gautam Kirtane
Author Photo: Ashwini Udgaonkar
Cover Design: Paridhi Rathore
Cricket player silhouettes: Deepu

CinnamonTeal Print and Publishing,
Plot No 16, Gogol, Housing Board Colony, Margao, Goa-403601
http://cinnamonteal.dogearsetc.com

Raj:

It is a pleasure to watch you play and an even greater joy to play alongside,

Best,

Vikram

Not Just Cricket...

VIKRAM DRAVID

CINNAMONTEAL
PUBLISHING

To all the strong women in my life

Acknowledgements

I would like to thank Jayapriya Vasudevan, Ramona Parsani and others at Jacaranda for their encouragement and editorial help.

Leonard Fernandes, Priyanka Pereira and others at Cinnamon Teal for getting this out in print.

Nirmala Subramani, Geeta Rao, Manjiri Prabhu, Varsha Bajaj, Ashwini Udgaonkar, Chitra Teredesai, Tahir Maqsood, Gauri Kirtane-Vanikar, Josy Paul and Leela Jacinto for reading the manuscript and providing invaluable insight.

Toby, my chocolate labrador, patient listener and sounding board.

Most of all, my family for believing and putting up with me.

Prologue

The click of the snick overrode the ambient cacophony as the ball flew off the edge. The game proceeded in slow motion. He turned to watch the ball. The seam rolled hypnotically. The images in his brain whirred and turned along with it. They kaliedoscoped and settled. The jigsaw puzzle jiggled, but stayed clear. The ball glanced off the tippy tips of the lunging hapless Nasir and sped towards thirdman. Arjun charged down the pitch as the ball careened towards the ropes. A sprinting Shohail raced around the arc and was airborne in a desperate dive. The ball took an awkward bounce and the desperate Shohail flailed at it, outstretched hand extended towards speeding orb. The hoardings lining the boundary seemed to converge on the ball. The small speck was indistinct in the melee as Arjun grounded his bat and turned around for a second run. The sunlight, the noises, the faces, the past, the present and the future all came together in a shining incandescent glow and he felt no more. Saw no more. Pandemonium erupted as the crowds emptied onto the field.

1

 It was no different from any other day. The ageless bustling suburb of Dadar had just settled down after the midday meal. Most of the inhabitants braved the afternoon heat under dusty whirring fans, attempting to digest a largely excessive mango-laden meal. The early afternoon quiet in 'Mangalya Dham', a middle class housing society was rudely interrupted by the sound of a shattered windowpane. Pallavi looked up interestedly from her book, her brother Arjun and his friends dispersed like fertilizing spores in the wind and peered around the graying corners of the building waiting for the inevitable eruption. They did not have long to wait.

'*Melanyo! Kartyanyo!* You have become such big *ghodas*, yet you play in the building. The society secretary has told you to go to the *maidan*. Arjun, I know you are hiding with that Sathe brat. Come on out. I want to talk to you. Wait till I tell your parents. Who is going to pay for this window?'

Mrs. Gadkari finally stopped her caterwauling and took in a deep breath. She brushed aside an errant hair that dared to obscure her vision. Arjun stepped forward sheepishly, 'But, there is a game on at the gymkhana, they won't let us play,' he offered conciliatorily. He swallowed hastily to gain courage and continued, 'And we have a game tomorrow. We have to practice.' Mrs. Gadkari's nostrils were flaring and rage was writ large on her sweaty brow. Arjun's explanation was futile, , the words rolling past her ears like water off a duck's back.

'Who is going to pay for my window? And all the others?'

She gazed balefully at her newspapered windows. The yellowing newsprint chronicled various battles lost by the panes.

'Here everyone thinks they are Suchen!'

She simmered down a bit pausing to drape her *pallu* and wipe her brow. Arjun mustered up some courage and looked like he was about to speak, but swallowed his words at the last moment. The other boys slunk around him like a pack of sullen dogs.

'Can we have our ball?' feigning insouciance, he finally mumbled.

The words had left his mouth but barely had time to settle. That was enough for a fresh tirade. Having regained her wind Mrs. Gadkari launched forth, 'BALL! You want your ball? I will show you a ball. How dare you? Are you going to leave or should I come down and convince you?'

At the prospect of a more intimate battle Pallavi finally put her book down and adjusted her glasses to a more comfortable position on her ever so slightly hooked nose, that interrupted an anciently beautiful face.

'Alright, alright,' Arjun muttered. He then turned to his partners in crime and whispered confidently, 'I will get it later.'

The boys collected their ragged gear, torn gloves, tired pads with belts replaced by muddy plaid handkerchiefs and assorted bats, stumps and balls. Now certain that the action was shifting venue, Pallavi ran down the stairs and joined the boys.

'Where are you going? To the gymkhana? Wait for me,' she wailed plaintively.

Troubled by the loss of yet another ball and more importantly an interrupted session of cricket, Arjun's forehead was furiously furrowed. His reply was definite, uncompromising.

"We are heading off. You catch up.'

The children trooped down the road and broke up into smaller groups. Pranay put his hand on Arjun's shoulder to commiserate the loss of the ball.

'She probably sells them! Say goodbye to that ball!' he proffered and getting a sudden visual of Mrs. Gadkari uncomfortably wedged on a commodious sofa amongst ever growing mounds of chilli-red balls, chuckled, 'I don't know how she has place to stay in her flat, with all those balls!'

Rahim caught up with them from behind and grabbed Arjun's hand demanding his attention, '*Saala*, you had one lucky shot today. I would have cracked your skull or at least a rib, if that witch had not saved you,' he sneered.

Unperturbed, Arjun retorted, 'If I would have hit your ball any harder, it would have exploded like a firecracker.' He mimed the exploding ball with exaggerated arm motions.

Not amused, Rahim shoved Arjun away. Pranay stepped between them with some timely advice, 'Why don't you save your energies for the field? Rahim, we are playing your team tomorrow. Guess it will be pretty evident who is better then.' Rahim contorted his face in a fierce scowl and walked away allowing himself a menacing look over his shoulder.

As they neared the *maidan*, Arjun gave his thought to matters at hand. The upcoming game, the next day. He turned to his friend somberly, 'You better have a good innings tomorrow. I can't guarantee anything. You know me, hit out *ya* get out! *laga to laga, nahi toh!*'

Suddenly serious, Pranay entered captain mode, 'I wish you would be more serious about your game. You have talent in spades, why can't you work on your application? Every ball can't be hit, you know! Be patient, pay attention to the fundamentals. You have a good eye....' Pranay's monologue threatened to get even preachier.

'As if I am planning to become a test cricketer,' Arjun cut him short.

Hurt at his advice being discarded nonchalantly, Pranay persevered.

'A little application would not hurt. Trying to do your best at any level....'

Arjun waved his hand impatiently to stem the monsoon-like torrent of words, '*Arre* enough lecture *baaji*. Now, walk quickly. I wonder who is playing at the gymkhana today. Should be a good game, there is a big crowd. We probably won't be able to play.'

Resigned to just watching the game, the boys tried to find a gap in the crushing crowd to move to the front. The crowd lined the tree fringed ground about five deep. An air of anticipation was apparent and unintelligible excited chatter was everywhere. Pallavi ran up panting, 'You could have waited! I was right behind you. Who's playing?' The words tumbled out, competing with deep indrawn breaths into her stressed lungs.

Without as much as a look in her direction, Arjun bounced on his tippy toes and telegraphed informatively.

'Trying to find that out.' Looking away he tugged at the sleeve of a severe looking man intent on blowing the most perfect smoke rings. 'Uncle *kaun khel raha hai?*' His concentration destroyed, the last ring looking distinctly triangular, the young man looked at the kids irritably.

'MIG ki team hai. Bol rahen hai ki Suchen khelne wala hai!'

SUCHEN! Suchen was GOD! At the prospect of watching the premier batsman in the world display his awesome skills, Arjun excitedly yelled, 'Suchen! Let's get to the front.'

Pallavi stood back, daunted by the wall of humans in front of her. Her darting eyes looked for a cleft, but chinks were nebulous; appearing and closing up like tricky visuals in a video game.

'Follow me!' Arjun urged, running away from the crowd and the game. His conflicting actions and excited tone confused his comrades.

Bewildered, Pranay shouted, 'What? Where are you going? I don't want to miss this.'

Arjun's confident stride beckoned his friends. Pranay and Pallavi followed, the others hesitated and then stayed put, looking for some high ground for enhanced viewing. The sprinting boys rushed into a nearby building. Pallavi's barely normalised breathing was ramped up again, as her burning lungs protested. A chilly sense of foreboding murmured to her, 'You know you are going to regret this.' She shut it out and tried to keep pace. The boys scaled a wall with ease; Arjun forged ahead, Pranay stopped to give Pallavi a hand. Recovering from the drop that left them on their haunches they found themselves running beside train tracks.

A local train, bulging at the seams with faceless populace, rushed by with a loud clatter. Passengers hung out of crowded doorways, hair and clothes blown askew by the wind; eyes screwed up to thwart determined and ubiquitous dust particles from finding a way into the welcome moisture within the eyelids.

The breeze in the wake of the screaming train almost knocked them over. The children crouched down, gasping, allowing the train to pass. Arjun excitedly pointed to a spot and clambered up a wall. Pranay helped Pallavi up and then perched himself next to her on the wall.

The kids were just behind a ramshackle shed, which served as a clubhouse and changing room for the players. They now had an unimpeded view of the game, placed slightly square of the wicket. The buzz from the crowd swelled as the lanky seamer charged in to bowl. Pranay could not contain his excitement,

'This is great! This is fantastic!'

As the kids settled in, leather found timber. They looked up to see stumps awry and a batsman headed dejectedly back to the shed. A roar went through the crowd, escalating in pitch and frenzy, a wave of anticipation and veneration brought the gathered faithful to their feet.

Suchen walked out to bat. His stride was purposeful as ever as he turned to squint into the sun, blinking to parcel into aliquots the onrushing blazing sunrays. He went through his usual rituals before taking guard and patting his left pad to adjust it to a more comfortable position. There was nothing in his demeanor to suggest that this was not as important a game as any. Always one to state the obvious, Pallavi yelled, 'It's Suchen. Suchen look here.'

Pranay was disapproving. 'Sshh! Don't disrupt his concentration.' Arjun looked at him scornfully, 'Like he cares about a local club game.'

Pranay bristled and retorted indignantly, 'Then he would not turn out for it! Now just watch, if you don't mind!' Suchen took his stance and spent a few moments looking around the field. He heuristically practised a few drives, changing the inclination of his bat ever so slightly each time.

The bowler who had just recently been jubilant, celebrating his success with high fives and up thrust arms now looked petrified. He charged in to bowl and sent down a rank bad long hop. Suchen patted the ball right back to him. The grateful bowler, confused but thankful, fumbled the ball before picking it up. But that was to be his only pleasant memory of the game. His next four balls were belted to various corners of the field, including a six that sailed right over the kids' heads. Pallavi adroitly jumped down from her perch and threw the ball back to the fielder.

The opposing captain brought himself on, at least partially to be able to tell his grandchildren that he had bowled to the great one. Against the flow of play, the ball crashed onto the stumps. Suchen was out, and the captain's story for his yet to be born grandchildren just got better.

Suchen walked back obviously dismayed with his momentary lapse of concentration. He entered the shed; the kids heard him noisily discard his kit. Their ears burned with the obscenities wafting up to them. An irate Suchen walked out, looking for a suitable bush to relieve himself. As he unzipped, he looked up and caught sight of the kids. Hastily zipping up he yelled, 'Hey! What are you kids doing here? A little privacy please.'

Disgustedly he looked around, picked up his gloves laid out in the sun to dry and threw them at the kids. The awestruck children kept gazing at their hero as the gloves sailed over their heads. Suchen shook his head in disbelief at the unmoving children and ambled back into the shed. The gloves meanwhile had settled down next to the train tracks. Still numbed by the first person interaction with GOD and unwilling to return to reality, Arjun jumped down reflexively and grabbed the sweat starched accessories. He pulled back as the urgent shriek of a rumbling train jarred the children back to *terra firma*. The train thundered by. Distraught, Pranay grabbed Arjun's sleeve urgently and pulled him further back.

'*Sala!* You could have been killed!' he hissed. Still unwilling to inhabit the planet of his birth, Arjun gazed at the gloves in his hands and said, 'I've got Suchen's gloves!' Not quite believing himself he repeated. 'I'VE GOT HIS GLOVES MAAN.'

A tinkle from the other side of the wall suggested that their hero had found an appropriate specimen of camouflaging vegetation. A panicky Suchen benevolently yelled, 'You can keep them. Just don't climb back onto the wall!'

Arjun grabbed the gloves and held them close to his bosom, 'You heard him! They are mine. I can keep them.' Another train shrieked by. The children cowered down; a frightened Pallavi said in a tremulous voice, 'I don't think it's safe to be here. *Aai* would be really angry if she knew we were by the railway tracks.' Pranay agreed, 'Let's go! Anyway Suchen is out.'

Pranay and Pallavi darted ahead. Arjun brought up the rear admiring the gloves, which were soiled, stained and still damp with Suchen's sweat.

Back on the landing of their building, they regrouped on a balcony carefully avoiding the betel-juice spit stained walls and examined the gloves more closely. Scarcely believing their luck they were whispering furtively when a broad shadow fell across the landing. A nosy Rahim walked up even as Arjun desperately tried to hide the gloves. Rahim tried to pull Pranay and Pallavi apart, as they attempted to cover a cringing Arjun who looked around for a good hiding place.

'What are you hiding?' Rahim demanded an answer. 'Show me?' He lunged forward pushing Pranay and Pallavi aside roughly.

'Oouch!' said Pallavi, clutching her forearm.

Arjun made a dash for the other side of the landing, but Rahim cut his path with a light-footed sidestep. 'What's that behind your back?' The now incensed Rahim queried as he grabbed Arjun and turned him around.

'These!' he said incredulously, 'These stinky old gloves? Why were you hiding them? I have a new pair, much better!' He volunteered this to the other hangers on. Relieved, Arjun remarked,

'Then you don't need these. Give them back please!' His interest now piqued, Rahim examined the gloves again.

'What's so special? Let me look at them.' Grabbing at them Arjun hastily said, 'Nothing!'

'Nothing!' echoed Pranay.

'Nothing at all!' a firm affirmation from Pallavi. Rahim looked at the three slyly.

'Nothing?' 'Ya! Nothing.' confirmed Arjun.

Rahim smiled, 'Alright then, I'll throw them away.' Arjun grabbed at the gloves again.

'No!' he cried. Rahim looked at him quizzically, 'No?' Pallavi had a brainwave,

'They have sentimental value!'

Happy to concur, Pranay chimed in, 'Yes, sentimental value!'

Not quite convinced Rahim asked,

'What sentimental value? Somebody speak up.'

His eyes darted from one face to the other. The three look at each other. If Rahim knew the gloves once belonged to Suchen, he would definitely keep them. Rahim held the gloves over the ledge.

'Speak up or get ready for a sentimental farewell.' The three looked at each other, ineffectual words formed in their minds and threatened to bludgeon their way out of their mouths. Their lameness was apparent and with sorrowful restraint the children stayed silent. Rahim looked at each one in turn. Finally, not getting a response he resignedly and deliberately dropped the gloves, one at a time. They landed on a parapet ten feet below. The three looked at them despondently, as Rahim walked away with the air of one having concluded a job well. The hangers on gasped. Rahim enjoyed that.

That evening Mr. Athavale walked back tiredly. The weary hiss of a stopping BEST bus was an apt sound byte for the spent evening. His walk was weary, but his eyes were bright and his face flushed. There was a happy wobble to his step, a result of having stopped for a quick one at 'Casbah', the local watering hole. This was not unusual for Mr. Athavale. As life had progressed he found it increasingly difficult not to give in to the winking neon-lit sign. The familiar comfort of the motley crew that gathered there each evening had given wing to his now increasingly inventive rationalization. After acknowledging all the frequent flushed faces, with a tinge of despair, for was this not an indication that he was here way too often Mr. Athavale, occupied a corner table and nursed his liquor without as much as another look around the bar. He was assured service and on dry days he was served in opaque steel glasses. One did not turn away a loyal patron. Actually, that particular day, it had been more than just one. A few gulped down quickly. A watchful eye on his ticking wristwatch, surely a greater time away from home, would be questioned more closely?

He slowly climbed up the steps to his apartment. The tired yellow light from a naked bulb barely lit his path; it left the edges and corners unpenetrated. Making the final turn, he found Mrs. Gadkari waiting on the landing. Reflexively he covered his mouth. A bumbling attempt to thwart any escaping vapors; though he had taken a few bites of a pungent raw onion to hide any odor. His proclivity for spirits was well known, however the agitated old lady had no time to dwell on his ongoing affair with Bachus. Setting pleasantries aside, she sallied forth.

'That brat of yours! Broke another of my windows today. What has happened to discipline? All of you...!' This, with a large gesture,... 'are content to let your progeny run wild. If you did not want to care for them, why did you have the damn brats? Now the wind and rain will come right in.'

At Mr. Athavale's quizzical look, she clarified. 'Through the broken windows; I hope you plan to get it fixed.'

His parenting skills in question, rage welled up but fatigue prevailed. All Mr. Athavale could come up with in reply was; 'It's summer. More air is refreshing *na!*'

The perceived levity of his tone and the now telltale whiff of liquor infuriated the worked up widow even more.

'You think it is a joke. Only I know how a poor widow like me has to juggle her finances to make ends meet. Now if Mr. Gadkari... may god give his soul everlasting peace. Now if Mr. Gadkari were around, these youth would not be running around unsupervised. I am sure he would have made certain that they were properly respectful! But who cares about a poor widow.' Intent on avoiding a prolonged conversation, Mr. Athavale replied, 'I will talk to Arjun.'

Not quite done, Mrs. Gadkari went on.

'You will have to do more than that. I am going to bring it up at the next society meeting.'

With a tired air of finality, Mr. Athavale countered, 'I am sure all the members will be most sympathetic.' He deliberately slid by the irate woman and strode towards his flat. His wife responded to the urgent jangling of the doorbell and let him in. He cast one last fearful look over his shoulder. Catching his eye, Mrs. Gadkari shook her fist at him. He hurriedly shut the door.

Later that evening, the family was gathered around the dining table. Arjun looked fidgety, his mind was obviously not on the food in front of him. Mr. Athavale pored over the newspaper while Pallavi adjusted her seat to get a better view of the overly loud television. Mrs. Athavale had lit the evening lamp and an incense stick lazily lived out its life before a multitude of randomly framed pictures of beatific gods and goddesses.

Jyoti Athavale bustled about fixing the evening meal. She walked over with a hot *chapatti*, 'Now, who would like this one?' she asked, beaming at her family.

Mr. Athavale looked up from the newspaper and set his glasses aside. Seeing his son reminded him of his tryst with Mrs. Gadkari. In his best stern voice, he asked, 'So you broke another window. Why can't you go to the *maidan*? This cricket nonsense infuriates me. Where is it going to take you? Have you given that any thought? Your time would be better spent in some more meaningful pursuits. First it was Naru, now you.' Driving a wedge in the unremitting tirade, Arjun interjected; 'But baba...!'

Not in the mood for an explanation or for that matter an interruption, his father continued.

'No buts. That Mrs. Gadkari is going to get a lawyer soon to sue us.'

Forever the peacemaker, his wife brushed her hair back with the back of her *atta* streaked hand. She volunteered, 'He is just a boy. If he won't play, who will? Accidents happen. Children have to expend their energy *na*. Can we not have any unpleasantness at dinner?'

In full flow now, her husband hammered his point home.

'Jyoti, if he has to play, can it be without destroying somebody's property? What's wrong with the *maidan*? Let him expend his energy there. Or maybe more ENERGY with the books. Ah! Well! That would be a refreshing change! I have not forgotten his last report card. Now if he was a dud I would not push him. Mr Dabholkar says he underachieves and takes pride in doing so. What bothers me most is that he is capable of so much more. Pallavi here never disappoints.'

At this Pallavi took a mental bow, but had a full-fledged preen cut short by a withering look from her brother.

'And Arjun here is much more intelligent.'

The deflated Pallavi mustered her best hurt look. Turning his seething eyes on his son, he thundered;

'You JUST WON'T TRY. Nothing is serious. Life is a pastel dream to waft through. Do you even think seriously about cricket? One day you will have to wake up and smell the shit... no roses....just....'

'ENOUGH...' Jyoti tearfully hissed.

'And this preoccupation with cricket; where did that get Naru?' Mr. Atavale finished, sputtering.

The last climactic pronouncement suggested that his father was done, at least for the moment. Silence may have been the best ploy, given the intensity of emotions, but Arjun defended.

'But baba, I need to practice. The inter-schools will be done in a month and then I will study. I promise. I will get it all done. And Naru, he was good, would have made Ranji atleast, ..I think.'

Feeling the need to have the last word, his father replied, 'There is no law against doing both at the same time. You talk about cricket as though you are going to be the next Suchen. And I don't want to talk about Naru.' The discussion was over. With an air of finality he turned his attention back to the newspaper, sliding his chair out to give himself room to cross his crisp pyjamaed legs. In a moment he set the paper down and held his head. Pallavi looked distressed at the strife. Having had quite enough and sensing that any further escalation could have a disastrous outcome, Mrs. Athavale said in a lower tone.

'*Aata puray ho!* Enough now. No more ugliness at the dining table or else you will both get indigestion. Another *chapatti*? No one tells me if the food is good or not!'

As if on cue the family looked at each other and replied in unison, 'Very good! Wonderful! Just like the Taj Mahal hotel.' Pleased, despite herself, the matriarch blushed, 'Like any of us have or will ever eat there! If you are done help me clean up, Pallu.'

That night, Arjun lay in bed, one arm curled below his head. Awake, staring at the ceiling. His mother quietly opened the door. Arjun looked up. Seeing her son awake; she walked in and sat on the side of the bed. She pulled the thick patterned sheet over him and smoothened out some creases in the coarse yellow fabric. Arjun slid over making more room for her. She slowly ran her hands through her son's unruly mane.

'He means well you know. He only wants the best for you.' Her voice was quiet and soothing, blending mellifluously with the muted night sounds.

Nudging his head closer to his mothers lap, Arjun pursed his lips and looked unconvinced.

'But he is never satisfied! I don't think I can ever perform up to his expectations. And why bring up Naru, what does that have to do with me?'

Mrs. Athavale gently interrupted, 'He is… uh… was your brother. It has been hard on your father. I am sure he will be happy if you just try your best at everything you do.'

Arjun still had his doubts. He looked up at the whitewashed ceiling with its sonorous, creakily persistent fan. Lost in thought for a moment he looked back at his mother.

'Do you really think so?' he asked.

His mother nodded and replied firmly, 'Yes! And shouldn't you sleep now? Don't you have that important match tomorrow?'

Arjun shut his eyes, his mother sat there for a few moments stroking his hair, looking down at him fondly. Finally she gathered herself up wearily and walked away. Arjun waited for a few minutes after the light in the other room had been turned off. He then opened his eyes and slowly looked around. A sudden clatter announced a cloudburst, a scary peal of thunder followed and a streaking bolt of lightening was the exclamation mark. Arjun raised himself onto one elbow and whispered in his sister's direction, 'Pallu! Are you awake?'

A gentle snore suggested otherwise. Summoning up his courage, he ventured a decibel louder, 'PALLU!'

The cobwebs of somnolence lifted. Pallavi stirred and then finally awoke.

'Huh! What!'

This was her best conversational effort; creditable given the hour and the depth of her slumber. She rubbed her eyes and felt around the head of the bed for her glasses while Arjun continued urgently.

'I need to get those gloves?'

Now completely awake, the conviction in her brother's voice promised an eventful night. She hoped to suggest caution by countering, 'Now?'

Undaunted, Arjun continued, 'Yah! We have the match tomorrow. I want to use them there.'

'It's raining. You probably won't play.' The hopeful voice of reason suggested.

Arjun was already changing out of his nightclothes, a deep, distant rumbling reminded him of the thunderstorm outside and he reached behind the door and grabbed his raincoat.

'Of course we will! In Bombay we are used to rain. Besides I am going to need all the help on a sticky wicket!'

Quite accustomed to giving in to the will of her single-minded and determined sibling, Pallavi stood up.

'Are you going to keep talking till I agree to help you?'

'Yes!' Arjun replied brightly. His eyes shone brightly in the blue half light of the room. His hurried movements cast a myriad of hasty shadows that darted across the walls in contorted confusion. Pallavi grabbed a shawl and an umbrella and charged after him.

'Then let's go!'

The two furtively crossed the expanse of the living room and with an ease that could only have come with practice, opened the usually squeaky front door without an audible sound. They sneaked down the hallway after carefully wedging a shoe to prop the door open. The air had cooled considerably with the downpour and the grateful parched earth had let out a contented belch of earthy smells.

They reached the landing and peered over the rusty railing. The gloves lay alongside a few banana peels and cigarette butts. They were soaked. Arjun looked down at them, there was a ten-foot drop and the parapet was fairly narrow, barely two feet wide and sloping ominously towards its edge. The persistent rains had added a film of treacherous green moss, which glistened portentously.

He picked up a bamboo stick from the corner used by the *bais* to hang clothes to dry. He dangled it over the railing trying to control the flailing stick while attempting to push the gloves over the edge. The bamboo was just a bit too short and made ineffectual sweeping arcs above the gloves. Arjun perilously leaned over even more to gain a few more inches. Suddenly Arjun's eyes were drawn to a drainpipe that ran along side the parapet.

An alternative route, a new plan.

He resolutely put the stick aside. Pallavi followed his stare, horror writ large upon her countenance, as she comprehended his plan. Futility apparent in her voice, she pleaded, 'No Arjun! You are going to fall.'

She already regretted getting shanghaied into this midnight caper.

Already clambering over the railing, Arjun replied matter-of-factly, 'I have no choice. *Aai* will never let me climb down tomorrow. I have got to get them now.'

Panic stricken Pallavi peered through the rain at the now sorry appearing gloves, 'Why? Now they are dirty and soaked.'

A voice already sounding distant, patiently and patronizingly explained, 'Well then I am going to have to dry them tonight. I want them for tomorrow's game.'

Before Pallavi could say any more, he reached over and grabbed onto the pipe. As if on cue, the rain intensified and a deafening clap of thunder drowned out a piercing scream from Pallavi as Arjun struggled to grip the mossy pipe, his dangling legs searching for a foothold. After a few precarious nerve-wracking moments, he regained his equilibrium and equanimity and surely shinned down the pipe, easily swinging himself onto the obsidian surface of the parapet.

'Got them!' he yelled up victoriously, the pelting rain forcing him to raise an arm to protect his eyes. Looking down he reached towards the gloves.

A bolt of lightening streaked down and electrified the gloves and his hands in a surreal blue haze. This time, Pallavi's scream was heard above the following peal of thunder, briefly interrupting Mrs. Gadkari's dream of the sun and moon alternately reflected in clear, shiny glassy windows.

The moment passed and as if on cue the rain abated. Arjun looked at the gloves incredulously, stuffed them into his waistband and climbed up the pipe. Pallavi looked on nervously and rushed to him as he climbed back over the ledge. After a hasty hug the two rushed back to their flat. Arjun placed the gloves under the fan to help dry them quickly and changed out of his soaked clothes. He crawled into bed and was soon breathing regularly, a content sleep.

The next morning, Arjun and his father walked towards his school. Arjun was dressed in spotless whites and carried a kit bag. His father's shabby briefcase made the old kit bag actually glow in comparison. Father and son stepped aside to allow a bevy of colorful fisherwomen walk by, rattan baskets filled with the day's catch, on ice, fluid leaking through the crevices as they hurried noisily to get their wares to the bazaar. The morning air was still and flies buzzed around impatiently. The deluge from the night had been soaked up by the ground, leaving behind a *sambar* thick mugginess. The sides of the road were occupied by frothy streams of gurgling water the color of freshly brewed coffee. The trees looked spotless having shed their dust and the sun had not yet commenced its assault. Gruffly clearing his throat, his father ventured conversationally, 'So whom are you playing today?'

Unusually intense and preoccupied, Arjun replied, 'King George.' Encouraged, Mr. Athavale continued, 'Do they have a good side?'

Arjun couldn't resist a snort at his father's naiveté. 'I should think so. They only won the shield last year! Looks like another first round exit for us.' Disgustedly his father turned to him, 'With that attitude I can guarantee it! With negativity there is never any hope. And without hope there is no effort. You need to believe that you can win. You can always win. Buy into that first, then give it your best. Otherwise, why even play? Just forfeit. As the unforgettable Lala used to say,

'Cricket is a game of glorious uncertainties',' Arjun interjected, 'And no match is won or lost till the last ball is bowled. Yaa-di-yaa-da. Yah! Right dad! Thanks anyway!'

The school gates loomed to his left abruptly. Eager to join his mates, Arjun turned without a formal goodbye and walked in. Mr. Athavale stood in place for a few moments gazing after him, fondly. Finally he shrugged; his thoughts indecipherable as he walked away. He missed Arjun's belated guilty wave.

The local train pulled into Victoria terminus, now rechristened, as most other British named edifices in Bombay/Mumbai as the Chatrapati Shivaji terminus. Arjun's father often joked, 'First Mahatma Gandhi was ubiquitous; every city had a MG road. Now in Bombay one can travel from the Chatrapati Shivaji terminus to the Chatrapati Shivaji airport on Chatrapati Shivaji road.'

The neo-Gothic structure built in 1888, with its ornate arches and domes and gargoyles suspended high above a timeless city didn't seem any different with a new name. And the city it overlooked, bustled on, unfettered by policies, prejudice or the peculiar political proclivity for particular personality promotion. Arjun and his teammates were oblivious to the ornamented panoply of arches, spires and domes high above them, as they made their way through congested heavy traffic. They had to fight for every inch of road space with honking cabs and exhaust-spewing trucks.

They heaved a sigh of relief as they finally gathered outside a tent on Azad *maidan* glancing nervously at the opposing team. Many games were due to commence at the same time and the field was spotted with youngsters in crisp cricket whites. Bougainvilleas spilled over the walls of adjacent buildings in naïve exuberance and brought a riot of colour to the periphery. The workforce hurried purposefully by.

The King George team looked quite professional, briskly tossing a cherry red shiny ball amongst themselves. They had their navy blue newly issued county caps on at rakish, jaunty angles. A throng of supporters was in attendance and announced their rabid support by cheering every bit of nifty ball handling being exhibited by their team. Pranay announced the obvious conversationally, 'Here come the umpires. I think we should field if we win the toss.'

That remark jarred his catatonic teammates out of their trance. Arjun was the first to retort, 'Against King George?' He paused for effect, rolling his eyes. 'We may not bat at all. Better bat first, so if we get out for a low score, they could get the runs quickly and we would not have to field forever.' Pranay glared at him, chastising him for his diffidence.

'Listen guys, we are all like fingers, not very effective alone. But ten together make two tough fists.'

Arjun giggled. 'What about the eleventh?' he quipped.

Pranay smiled,'We need one extra finger to poke their eyes out, once we knock them down.'

Pleased with his own witticisms, he walked out to join his counterpart and the umpire. Just then Rahim left his teammates and strolled over to Arjun, '*Abey murgi*, I hope you are coming out to open, this sticky wicket will help me bloody your mouth!'

Arjun gulped and attempted a stony stare before looking away. Pranay returned from the middle, his team looked up at him expectantly. Pranay attempted a cheery tone,'I lost the toss guys. We field.'

He turned away from his groaning teammates and looked out at the *maidan* already teeming with activity, as games got underway at the multiple inter-lacing wickets. The umpires walked out and Pranay led his team out, shouting encouragements and exhorting grudging responses.

The first few overs were innocuous, the cautious openers, made the average seam attack seem more menacing than it really was. The batsmen eventually got adventurous and the scoreboard rattled on, till the clatter of timber signaled the fall of a wicket. Just as Arjun's team was ready to throw in the towel, a wicket fell. This was a harbinger of things to come. Although runs were scored, the vaunted King George batting lineup flattered to deceive, finding ways to lose wickets against an insipid bowling attack made to look even worse by lackluster fielding. However, as soon as there had been a few cracking boundaries, the odd skier found itself stuck in somewhat reluctant hands.

The fall of the sixth wicket signaled the arrival of Rahim. Obviously a crowd favorite, he walked in with a swagger that demanded the roar of applause and anticipation that greeted him. As if to appease his fans he belted the seamers to distant corners of the *maidan*. The distressed fielders now definitely believed that the worst was yet to come. When Pranay brought himself on, Rahim could not believe his eyes, heaving his slow spinners for two sixes. The next ball was flighted even higher and took its time descending from the skies. Manna from heaven. Brimming with confidence Rahim made room and smacked an inside out shot over cover against the spin. The ball swerved in the air as Arjun dashed towards it and finally made a great one handed catch on the boundary. With the unbelieving look of a gourmand interrupted in the midst of his favorite repast, Rahim returned to the tent. He turned and glared at Arjun as the bedraggled fielders allowed themselves a minor celebration.

As if shocked by this turn of events, the remainder of the King George batsmen capitulated easily, making Pranay's innocuous spin look decidedly deadly. King George were all out for 192. Both teams retreated to the tent, settling down at separate tables for lunch that had been sent over from the respective schools. Rahim paused between mouthfuls of succulent *biryani*, 'You know I will get you for that.'

Always the level headed one, Pranay, the serious captain emboldened by his new found bowling prowess patted Arjun on the arm and turned to

Rahim, 'Why don't you just play the game?'

This was more a statement than a question. The umpires signaled resumption and the teams returned to the field. Arjun's team went in to bat and started disastrously. The listlessness evident while fielding was even more evident in their batting. Each member of the team had that 'deer in the headlights look' of being in a situation too big for them. Nobody questioned the eventual result. They were just going through the motions. Rahim bowled viciously and hit almost every batsman that walked out. The men wielding the willow weaved, ducked, jumped aside, fell flat on their behinds, took many a blow to their bodies and eventually got out. Pranay came in at the fall of the first wicket and played steadily, keeping one end up while the ugly display at the other end continued. The batsmen actually looked relieved at getting out.

At 90 for 8, Arjun walked in and Pranay walked over to him,

'Arjun! Just occupy the crease. Put a price on your wicket.'

Arjun looked up cynically, scorn writ large on his circumspect visage.

'And we will score a hundred runs! Get real!'

Trying to sound assured, Pranay continued, 'Now listen! No game is lost...'

'Till the last ball is bowled! I know! I know! Does everyone talk in clichés?' Arjun replied, his voice betraying his lack of conviction as he walked back to his crease shaking his head.

He didn't bother to take guard and tapped his bat impatiently. The first ball he received was a bouncer which took off steeply after pitching; he ducked under it, visibly shaken. The next was pitched up and he lofted it over Rahim's head for a four. Arjun looked down at his bat incredulously, thinking out aloud, 'How did I do that?'

The next few overs unfurled in slow motion, as if time itself realized that momentous happenings could not be hurried. Impervious to the cauldron like heat of the mid afternoon, Arjun unleashed an array of shots. His burgeoning strokeplay was savage, yet highlighted by some delicate cuts and deflections that bisected the gaps and raced to the ropes. Arjun could not stop himself from looking at his bat disbelievingly after every shot.

The roar of the crowd was muted and overpowered by the urgent screams of the sparse supporters for Arjun's team. The ingenuity of his batting, the sheer artistry of his strokes, the caliber of his timing left all viewers agape. Effortlessly the scoreboard moved onto 160 for 8. Pranay had kept his end up but did precious little else. At the end of an over the two met in the middle. Pranay felt the need to have some input as his team inched towards an improbable victory. Shaking his head, unable to suppress a smile Pranay said, 'I don't know how, but I like it. I like it. I LIKE IT! Don't change a thing. I didn't know you could play the reverse sweep.'

Arjun looked up, tapped the pitch with his bat and walked away, turning back to say, 'Neither did I.'

In the next over, anti-climactically Pranay was out lbw. The ball had hit the turf outside the leg as Pranay stretched forward to offer a dour pad. Disbelievingly he walked back, convinced that the decision had more to do with the fact that the umpire raising his ugly finger was currently digesting the always excellent *biryani* from the King George cafeteria; rather than the merit of the ball.

The last man walked out with ill-disguised nervousness. He occupied the crease with the bearing of an errant pigeon trying to avoid the menacing blades of a whirring fan while trying to find a way out of a room accidentally entered. As the burly bowler sped in to deliver, he edged towards square leg but somehow managed to push the ball away from the stumps. He stepped away and turned to look longingly at the sanctity of the tent. Its billowing canvas invited him like a mother's bosom to its fold.

'And that's over,' said the umpire.

At 166 for 9, 27 runs were needed for victory. The impossible, which had looked achievable for a bit, now seemed decidedly out of reach.

Rahim beckoned for the ball as he walked back to his long run up. Arjun toyed with the idea of formulating some plan with his teammate, then decided against it. One look at number 11 revealed his plan as he rearranged the dirt and loose bits of grass within the crease at the non-strikers end, intent on a prolonged stay away from the firing line. The fierce look on Rahim's face as he turned to bowl reinforced this simple survival strategy.

As Arjun looked up to receive the first ball from Rahim, a calm numbness descended over him. The activity and noises in the periphery retreated out of his consciousness. The first ball was short outside the off, Arjun gently tapped it late and helped it along the way to the fence. A smattering of polite claps from the tent suggested that his teammates felt that this was just a speed-bump on the way to eventual defeat. Rahim swung his arms over, made a few fielding adjustments and walked back to bowl. He dug the next one in short, the ball reared viciously towards Arjun's head. Scenting blood Rahim threw his hands up. A late flash of arcing willow inserted the top edge of the bat in the path of the ball which swerved off and lobbed over the shortest boundary behind the keeper. An unconvincing stroke but six runs nevertheless. Fuming, Rahim walked back and this time delivered an inswinging yorker. A quick step forward converted this into a full toss. The sweet sizzling straight drive whizzed past the frantic fingers of a lunging Rahim. Four more brought the tent to its feet.

The King George faithful were silent; mentally crossed fingers urged for deliverance from this unexpected first round struggle. Pranay rushed out, 'No hurry, Arjun! Get a single off the fifth or sixth".

Number 11 crossed his heart in his mind and sent up a silent prayer, putting in a plug for the sixth. Arjun apparently had other plans. The next two balls were of good length, deft footwork and steely wrists reduced them to longhops, dispatched contemptuously to the midwicket and cover boundaries. With the last ball of the over coming up, number 11 walked down the wicket and pleaded with Arjun to take a single.

At 188 for 9, 5 required for a win, Pranay was uncharacteristically animated and yelled detailed instructions. His voice was drowned by the excited chatter of his teammates. An air of expectancy spread over the field and other games paused, sensing a decisive moment.

The King George supporters, raucous through the majority of the game, were quiet, a collective holding of bated breath. Rahim trundled in and delivered a beautiful slower ball that cut in off the seam. Shaping for a cover drive Arjun quickly adjusted, his feet shuffling together in precise ballerina like movements. He sailed into the ball and lofted it majestically over long-off onto the road.

The umpire raised both hands in a staccato motion.

'SIX!'

Arjun charged back to the tent, fists pumping at having secured an unforeseen and eerily bizarre victory. The tent erupted into a melee of celebration. Unbridled emotion translated into a hodge- podge of unchoreographed movements. The chaos disrupted the tent pegs and the canvas gently settled on the manic team.

Later the tired boys walked away, heading to Churchgate to grab a quick snack before going home. The palm trees around the Rajabhai clock tower were gently swaying with visible rustling in the late evening wind as if in silent applause. Fashion Street bustled with haggling collegians trying to drive a hard bargain for ethnic jewelry and export reject clothing. There was a crowd outside Eros, lining up for tickets to view a new action filled Hollywood offering.

Pranay was unable to contain himself. He grabbed Arjun's arm.

'What just happened? How did you improve your concentration, stroke selection, footwork, timing, technique, and application all in one fell swoop? Do you have a fever? Did you go to the temple or something this morning?'

Back to his usual taciturn self, after the giddy merriment Arjun looked confused.

'I..I don't know.' 'It's got to be something'. 'If I did not know you, I would have said it was somebody else batting out there. You remember Naru and how he and that Ranji player...Patkar somebody... This was freaky, just like that!' Pranay persisted. His face lit up and he then added giggling, 'Did you see Rahim's face when you straight drove him?'

A smile creased Arjun's face.

'That was priceless. Yet, I wonder.......................'

Turning to confront his friend's troubled face Pranay said, 'Wonder what? What's on your mind? Come on *yaar*, you must tell me.'

Arjun looked down at his hands. 'I wonder if it was the gloves! Remember the gloves that Suchen tossed away yesterday. I batted with them today. Pranay, how could I improve drastically like that? Must be the gloves.'

The idea established residence in his mind like a determined squatter. He turned to Pranay and his face was alight with sudden enlightenment. He continued with conviction.

'It's gotta be the gloves.'

Pranay gave this statement an appropriately polite, brief thought before retorting. 'The gloves. THE GLOVES. Have you lost your mind? You really must be feverish. You have your gene pool in your favor. Naru almost made university, obviously you have some talent!'

He reached over and felt Arjun's brow. Shaking himself loose Arjun demanded an alternative explanation.

'What else can it be? I felt like I had no control. The bat moved like it was a wand. I was more surprised than anyone else! Even Naru never played this well.'

Appreciating the futility of continuing the discussion, Pranay sought to close further deliberation.

'Enough of this nonsense! For once you applied yourself and played to your true potential and you want to credit some grungy gloves for your success.'

Not to be deterred, Arjun retorted.

'Well, there is just one way to find out.' He leaned over and whispered his plan conspiratorially.

The next morning the boys met at the foot of the stairs of Arjun's building. It was a school holiday, but business as usual for the rest of the city. Skirting a carelessly parked bicycle, the boys looked around, allowing bustling *dabbawalas* the right of way as they picked up hot meals to be delivered to the workforce downtown. Once they were certain that they weren't being observed and there was nay a flutter even in the curtains of Mrs. Gadkari's newspapered windows, they walked stealthily around the corner of the building. Arjun carried a bat and gloves, THE GLOVES. Pranay twirled a ball in the air. They warily looked around again and after ensuring that they were alone Arjun tossed his gloves to the ground and took his stance. Neither was aware of a pair of hidden eyes taking in this tableau. Pranay tossed up a few flighted leg spinners. Arjun jabbed and missed the first few. Looking quite uncomfortable he finally heaved at a googly in frustration, missed it completely and fell to the ground. Getting up hurriedly he dusted himself off, walked over and put on the gloves.

Pranay returned to toss up a few more. A cover drive, a square cut, a divine on drive and finally a rasping straight drive followed. Both boys look stunned and approached each other circumspectly. Pranay was the first to speak.

'Tell me that you just did that on purpose. For a moment it was Naru batting out there. The way you tilted your head on that straight drive. You are spooking me!' Arjun looked as baffled as he grabbed the skin of his throat and blurted, '*Ma kasam*, I swear, I did not...I am as spooked as you!' Before they could discuss this turn of events any further, Rahim strode around the corner of the building. The loss from the day before, still smarted. Its memory brought up a fiery feeling at the back of his head. He felt compelled to flare his nostrils and snarl, 'What are you sissies whispering about? It won't make any difference. You aren't going to win the next round. Flukes like that don't happen all the time.'

With newfound confidence, Arjun could not resist.

'Want another go at me?' he taunted.

Pranay tossed the ball over to Rahim who did not hesitate for a bit and strode back purposively to his run up. He came charging in and dropped one just short of length. The ball reared up off the concrete. Arjun rocked back onto his back foot and pulled the ball. The three boys followed the parabola till another one of Mrs. Gadkari's panes rudely interrupted it. The sound of glass breaking shattered yet another peaceful interlude in Mangalya Dham and sent a few crows cawing and a solitary pigeon fluttering before it settled down to an indignant cooing. Her weekly hair bath rudely interrupted, the harried woman looked at the shards on her bathroom floor and erupted, '*Melyano*, now they are coming at me from all sides.'

Before she could peer out to discern the identity of the transgressors, the boys gathered up their stuff and ran away. The hidden eyes cautiously retreated.

FATE and DESTINY. The words jostled for space in Arjun's life. He was unsure about their exact meaning or import, but suddenly they seemed vital.

How did they relate to LUCK? To ABILITY? And was TALENT a little bit of all of them.

What does one do? What should one do? Accept inevitible FATE and irrevocable DESTINY and ride lady LUCK?

He remembered Savitri kaki's parable about Abhimanyu, the warrior prince and his tryst with Chakravyuha. They were all seated around her in a circle, gobbling dumplings of rice and dal lovingly fisted by her, listening, wide-eyed and attentive.

Arjun still felt the pang when he had first heard Savitri kaki describe Abhimanyu's end. Abhimanyu had been equipped to break into the Chakravuya. knowledge of which he had gleaned in his mother's womb, but did not know how to get out of it. After crashing through the formation, the brave lad was slain.

Was it FAIR? Why did Savitri kaki tell them that story? To highlight the inescapability of FATE or the COURAGE of the warrior prince? Would he, Arjun, face similar choices? How does one accept something that is beyond comprehension?

And Naru? What about Naru? FATE? LUCK? CHOICE?

These thoughts befuddled him off the field, but on the field he rode his purple patch.

NARU

The fierce sunlight assaulted their eyes as they walked out of the theatre. They felt the searing heat radiating from the baked asphalt a moment later. 'Bridge on the river Kwai' had always been a favorite. Alec Guinness' performance still awe inspiring. But Naru could relate the movie backwards even dwelling on subtle nuances. A combination of boredom and the enticement of air-conditioning blatantly advertised as 'every seat a cool retreat' had seen them amble into the movie a few hours earlier. In fact the early part of each day was spent in planning. The discounted morning shows or matinees were always a top option. Lackadaisical professors, making interesting subjects tedious by uninspired [I'm only doing this because it pays the bills, my job description does not require the use of creativity or imagination] instruction made certain that spending time in classes at medical college was not a practicable alternative.

They had made the required forays down Fashion Street and Colaba Causeway. They ogled at the food in various restaurants along the way. The used booksellers hawking everything from quantum physics texts to homegrown, crudely worded pornography were always an enticement. Now, time hung heavy, the heat ubiquitous and omnipotent, kept them on the move.

Nishit or No-shit as he called himself ['that's what I am because that's what I take, 'No-shit,' get it?' was the line he dropped on unsuspecting, first time, unfortunate female acquaintances; there had been no second time acquaintances of the fairer sex to date] suggested a quick bite.

The next half hour was spent on *pav-bhaji* and *kala khatta*, while admiring the majesty and intricacy of the Mumbai municipal corporation building. It staidly stood beside the more majestic railway terminus quietly confident of its own architectural virtues.

They decided to check out the new crop at Xavier's. Every June brought new, animated and pretty faces to the college. The guard checking identity cards had been bribed and waved them in with a salute. Two sugary teas later the meager canteen crowd could not hold their attention. They wandered out.

Nishit started talking about the inter-medical cricket match the next day, as he walked across the street neatly sidestepping unpredictable cars with nimbleness incongruous with his bulky build. Although academics had not grabbed centre-stage one year into medical college, cricket definitely had and they both had made the college side. Now their absences from mind-numbing classes were legitimized by the mention of 'nets', and a good performance on the field more than made amends for curricular shortcomings.

Nishit lit a cigarette from a smoldering rope that divested itself of a few embers and turned to see Naru bent over talking to a roadside astrologer who apathetically foretold usually bleak, and sometimes, hopeful futures with the help of his mangy parrot. He walked over and in an attempt to nip the prospective deal in the bud, let out an, 'Aw, c'mon yaar.' Naru proffered 'Just time-pass *yaar*' by way of explanation.

Now Naru was not into any of the mumbo-jumbo as he called it. When his mother had his palm read by Savitri *kaki* he made a big show of disbelieving, and proved her predictions of his being a wastrel wrong by securing a much-coveted spot in a prestigious medical college. In his world that wasn't as important, but his father's face, flushed with pride had suggested that it was the right decision. Right then, this man had caught his eye. He sat in a row of hawkers peddling their ware. Dhoti-clad men squatting on their haunches wielding rusty instruments that reminded one of medieval torture, cleaned ears. A few had neatly folded second hand clothes in piles for sale, while one stood nonchalantly drawing attention to two dolls that appeared to be magically entwined in an skippy jig. The other fortunetellers were occupied in daily chatter.

This man sat apart. A purple turban and a generous application of kohl could not draw attention away from intense smoky gray eyes. Without perceptible motion or emotion, the eyes seemed to beckon. More intrigued than mesmerized, Naru had walked over. Reading the sign asking for a rupee for his fortune, he reached into his pocket and put a coin down. The man deliberately let his parrot out of its cage. The scruffy bird walked over and hesitated a few times before unambiguously picking up a card with his beak. The man pried it away, fed the parrot a few seeds and scrutinized the card with squinted eyes and a creased brow.

'Good luck and fame can all change. In the midst of good fortune, bad times are just a stone's throw away.'

'What does that mean?' Naru inquired, 'Will I become a surgeon?'

The man looked up and deliberately repeated, 'Be careful?' He looked away indicating that the session was done. Naru almost protested that he had not got his money's worth, but something in the man's intensity and troubled brow held him back. He stood up and walked across the street.

'Bullshit, voodoo, mumbo-jumbo right,' Nishit volunteered. Naru nodded half-heartedly and turned back to look at the soothsayer. He was gone, like he had never been there.

They walked by the cricket stadium and saw that the doors had been thrown open for the final session. A paltry crowd of a thousand or so was watching a Ranji trophy game. People were leaving as they walked in; the scoreboard afforded the reason why. Mumbai was in the doldrums, the batsmen apparently without an answer to the turbaned Delhi off spinner's guiles. Delhi had amassed 382 in their first innings; Mumbai was 192 for 7 in reply on the penultimate day of the tie. The match was obviously going to be decided on first innings scores. Mumbai's current Mr. Reliable, Suresh Patkar was at the crease unbeaten on 54, the number 9 batsman was walking out to join him. The international luminaries of the star studded Mumbai batting had all failed, probably due to an inability to shift focus and intensity to a domestic tie.

Naru bought some roasted peanuts dexterously wrapped in yesterday's newspaper and they settled to watch the game. Patkar skillfully manned the strike and delivered some well-timed hits off the offie. The scoreboard kept moving. Number 9 began to believe in his batting abilities, albeit only the defensive ones and the game suddenly became an adsorbing duel. Naru and Nishit were agreed on the shortsightedness of the national selectors for having ignored the tremendous temperament of Patkar, which in their opinion more than compensated for any perceived deficiency in flashy stroke play. At close Mumbai were 298 for 7. Patkar had his hundred and Mumbai an outside shot at salvaging the game.

They walked towards Churchgate to get a train home. Their upcoming game the next day supplanted the game they had been watching in their minds and conversation. Nishit provided his own take on the best strategy. Naru listened halfheartedly, the day's events cascaded through his mind at the same time. Nishit left at Grant road, Naru proceeded to Dadar and slowly trudged home. Cricket was the conversation at dinner. Naru's father had his prophecies for the Ranji tie, with pointers about how each side could clinch victory. Naru had a troubled night, filled with dreams of batting on stony wickets, barefoot and running the gauntlet of brickbats each time he tried to take a run.

The next morning was sunny and bright, like the past many. Naru packed his kit in a grey well worn Air-India carry-on bag and took the train to Marine Lines and then walked over to Azad Maidan. Their opponent that day was the Government Dental College, a team propped up by one man,

Mehul Sanghvi. His exploits at the school level had many predicting an eventual Test cap. Age, injuries and the demands of a professional education had laid that to rest, but his immense talents were undisputed.

GDC batted first. Naru stood back, knocking his keepers' gloves together to get the right fit; his mind a restless churning of thoughts. He could not get the mystic out of his brain. Those smoky gray eyes seemed to be presiding over all in there. 'Click,' the sound of the snick brought him back. He saw the ball veering toward him, buzzing like a distraught bee. It seemed to stick to his glove before it ballooned out and dropped to the ground. 'Nice beginning,' opined the captain, 'Wake up!' this one from Nishit and finally Javid at first slip, not to be outdone, '*Saale, tu ne us ball ko dhool ka phool bana dala*'. Crestfallen Naru looked away.

Sanghvi, grateful for the first ball reprieve, took fresh guard and proceeded to make his opponents pay for their lapse. He dispatched the attack to all corners of the ground. The ferociousness of his pulls and hooks were only surpassed by the sublime timing of his late cuts. Wickets fell at the other end, but Sanghvi held his ground, carrying his bat for a well-made 127. GDC finished with 212 from 50 overs.

Lunch was a somber occasion; no one mentioned the dropped catch, but it lay heavy like a pall on their spirits.

'Let's go, let's go,' urged the captain by way of encouragement.

The medical college innings started disastrously, they lost Nishit and Javid in the first over. The captain then dug in and fashioned a recovery of sorts. When the fortieth over was completed, they needed 72 runs with 4 wickets in hand. The first ball of the 41st saw a tired captain fall to a lapse in concentration as he holed out to deep midwicket. As he disappointedly made his way back, shaking his head and pounding his bat into the turf, he stopped to counsel Naru walking in.

'You can do it, this is your chance to redeem yourself,' he advised, his tone belying his lack of belief in his own words.

Naru started cautiously pushing and prodding for singles, but almost immediately the medical college lost another wicket as the other set batsman was bowled. Number 10, a spidery thin fast bowler, who had an inflated opinion of his almost nonexistent batting talents joined Naru in the middle. Naru assumed the mantle of the senior batsman and began stroking the ball fluently, finding gaps. The lanky pacer kept him company till the 48th over; when, with 16 runs required to win and urged by yells of '*Maro, Maro,*' from the tent, he went for a heave and was castled. Chastising himself for his indiscretion and saddened by the unfinished task he gave way to number 11.

Now number 11's aversion to batting was probably the reason for number 10's unrealistic assessment of his own batting skills. Often number 11 failed to move both, bat and legs, as he watched turning balls and whizzing out swingers go by him. He jabbed nervously at the last ball of the 49th over and sighed with relief as the ball missed bat, pad, stumps and a surprised wicket keeper. Naru refused the proffered bye and took fresh guard for the last over.

The shouting from the tent rose to a crescendo as Sanghvi dropped his field back to save the boundaries. The first ball of the 50th whizzed past the flashing bat to the keeper, to a loud 'oooh' from the tent. Naru looked around circumspectly and slammed the next two deliveries for crisp cover driven fours. Sanghvi brought in an extra man in the deep, Naru danced outside the off and flicked the next ball for four more to square leg.

Two balls and four runs needed, number 11 bravely rehearsed strokes lest he be called to action. The tent looked eerily calm as its occupants spilled out onto the field and waved any piece of cloth they could get their hands on, shirts, towels and even jockstraps. Naru flicked the next ball through midwicket and charged down intent on picking up two runs to retain strike. Caught up in the exuberant pace of the moment, number 11 charged back for the third. Naru had to make a quick decision. Sending number 11 back would result in a definite run out. He set out and dived for the non-strikers crease as the bowlers attempt to guide the throw-in onto the stumps missed its mark by a whisker. The crowd heaved a sigh of relief that continued into a groan as they realized that number 11 needed to score off the last ball.

Sanghvi brought the field in to prevent the single. Number 11 attempted a brave, 'bring it on' look. The last ball was wide outside the off stump, number 11 flashed and missed, Naru charged down calling for the run. Number 11 was rooted to the spot and Naru reached the strikers crease. The keeper's lobbed throw flew past him. Number 11 finally got the plan and charged down and for a few agonizing moments there was a race between 11's leg-speed and the parabolic arc of the ball. 11 reached for the crease as the ball gently rolled onto the non-striker stumps lightly dislodging a bail which reluctantly succumbed to gravity in slow motion.

The fielders went up, hope writ large on their face.

OUT, decided the umpire.

A TIE, not as good as a win but definitely better than losing, particularly because the crucial point gleaned meant that they would play the finals.

Naru returned an unbeaten 52. There were subdued congratulations all around. The team then stopped at Rustam's icecream parlor for a celebratory ice cream. As Naru licked his butterscotch cone circumferentially he watched the flaming orb douse itself in the Arabian Sea. The gray eyes jumped to life in the back of his brain. He dropped his cone and looked around startled. He could have sworn that a swish of purple briefly obscured the sunset.

That evening a tired and flushed Naru plonked himself on the sofa after an excited dinner. The Ranji tie had slipped his mind. The day's happenings, and his own exploits occupied a large part of his cerebral crunching. A photograph of Patkar flashed on screen, as the newscaster monotonously droned.

'And Patkar's rearguard action finally ensured that Mumbai would tie Delhi's first innings score. Patkar remained unbeaten on 152, finishing the Mumbai first innings with three fours and a six. The last ball saw Mumbai lose their last wicket as the players tried to run a non-existent bye. But Patkar's heroics more than made amends for his dropped catch of first innings Delhi centurion Rakesh Lal. So Mumbai saves face and stays alive to fight another...'.

'Hey! That sounds just like your day Naru,' his father commented.

The similarities were undeniable and Naru smiled, 'Fortune favors the brave,' he chirped by way of elucidation.

The similarities didn't end there. It was as though their fortunes were tied, entwined. A good performance from Patkar was invariably associated with a similar showing by Naru. Both recorded first ball ducks on the same day and at the end of the week, Patkar's current season Ranji average and Naru's inter-medicals average were identical. This became a source of amusement to Naru's teammates and even his family. Javid loudly proclaimed that Patkar and Naru must visit the same temple, seeking benevolence from the same deity. Naru's father jokingly planned to open a bookie joint to take bets on their performances, as one's infallibly predicted the others.

One evening there was a piercing scream as Pallavi yelled, 'I don't believe it'. She pointed excitedly at The TV screen; Rabi Mantri was interviewing Patkar. 'That shirt... it's exactly the same one *da* is wearing. You two are getting freaky now.' The last pronouncement led to an admonishment from her mother as Naru compared his own shirt to Patkar's. Doubtless, they were identical.

Naru's teammates now really launched into him. Nishit, true to his name, innocently asked, 'What time did Patkar move his bowels today?' Javid suggested that life must be one big orgasm for Naru, given that Patkar was recently married and all that! Captain could barely hide his smile at these witticisms, but urged his team to focus on the game.

On the eve of the inter-medical finals, Naru and Nishit were walking towards the station. India's national side for the upcoming tour of the West Indies was to be announced that day. Both agreed that Patkar's domestic performances had guaranteed him a spot, but differed on whom the final spot in the fifteen should go to. Naru favored a seaming all-rounder, while Nishit opted for a third spinner.

'Kamble has stopped turning the ball *yaar*, if he gets whacked we will need another option.'

Naru offered, 'All-rounders are a key to a well balanced side, look at Botham, Sobers, Imran or even Kapil.'

'No argument, if we had one of them, but Adarkar... huh,' Nishit said disparagingly.

They clambered onto a crowded local, the clatter of the train and the din of many conversations at the same time made serious dialogue impossible. Nishit detrained at Grant Road, Naru made his way to the other side to get off at Dadar. Just as he was getting off, he felt a hand on his shoulder and heard the words, '*Bachke rehna, sambhalna* [take care, beware] whispered in his ear. Fighting the crowds to get out, feeling for his wallet and turning around to look for the source of the warnings, Naru felt again that he momentarily saw a swath of purple fabric moving into the crowd in the train.

That evening the Indian team was announced. Patkar replaced an out of form VVS Bharath in the side, which was no surprise. Adarkar was preferred to a third spinner. Naru sat in his balcony feeling strangely elated at Patkar's selection. Maybe there was something to this telepathic connection. His father returned from work with the late edition newspaper.

"Congratulations,' he yelled, walking in.

'Enough dad,' said Naru, 'I know Patkar got selected in the Indian side.'

"Who's talking about Patkar?' His father replied, 'Did you see the Mumbai university probables?'

'No, What about them?' Naru's curiosity was piqued. His father thrust a folded newspaper under his eyes, 'Whose name is this? Narayan Athavale... there, bold as mango stains on a white shirt.'

'Shit! I'm sorry, I didn't even know I was in the running,' Naru shouted. 'Besides I'll never make the team.'

'Nonsense,' his father firmly interjected. 'Isn't Patkar in the Indian side? What's good for the goose...' he continued metaphorically confused.

'Oh! Stop Dad! You are babbling. Coincidences are just that, coincidences. It's gotta stop, and I am predicting that here is where the similarities will end.'

'At least give it your best shot, you know my uncle once played with the famous CK Nayadu for the Holkars. After him, you have the opportunity to do justice to the family genes.'

The next morning Naru was late, Arjun hogged the lavatory and Pallavi sneaked in for a shower before him. The inter-medical finals were being played at the stadium and he didn't want to be late, though he doubted that the captain would drop him. The thought of the captain fretting and letting lose a few choice invectives at his late appearance brought a smile to his face.

Sporting a sunny countenance he made his way to the station, trying to get ahead of the plodding crowd. He waited on the bridge to catch the first available train and gleefully charged onto platform five as the fast train streamed in. He caught a brief look at the headlines on the sports page as a fellow commuter folded his newspaper in preparedness for the battle to get onto the train.

'Patkar out of Windies tour' the headlines screamed, 'Jugraj in' was the smaller strapline.

Why? He wondered, after working so hard for this chance, what was more important? His mind went over various scenarios, as the train pulled out of Dadar. He was hanging out the train as was his usual habit, it was cooler, most of the stations were on the other side and he was getting off at the last stop; Churchgate. The train rolled past Mahalakshmi, banking to his side, he gripped the upper ledge firmly, secured a better foothold and clutched his Air-India bag firmly. Looking into the train he saw a purple turban bobbing toward him. This was definitely more than a coincidence. Why was this man following him? Suddenly, those intense smoky grey eyes were on him. The eyes widened in anticipation and urgency. The clairvoyant lunged forward desperately in a bid to thwart fate. Seeing the advancing figure, Naru took a sudden sharp breath. It was his last. The brick hurled by the urchin struck him on his temple. He lost his grip and plunged out. His skull was split open by the electric pole. His last memory those grey eyes, and a hand attached lunging out to pull him back. The intensity in those eyes intent on denying their own prophecy.

By the time the chain was pulled and the train stopped, the urchin had grabbed the Air-India bag and disappeared. People jumped off the train and milled around the body. The purple turban was nowhere to be seen.

Sleeping in on a Saturday, Anand Athavale opened the newspaper, 'Rotten luck, this Patkar fellow has. Just when he was about to break into big time, he went and got hit on the head in the nets, with a bouncer. Do you know he was operated on last night? He will be OK. Don't know if he will have the confidence to bat again.'

The coincidences had ended; one death had sealed that.

At lunchtime during the intermedical finals, the medical college had done rather well, getting 273 for 6 in 50 overs. Nishit said, 'I hope Naru is OK. It's not like him to ditch at the last moment. Maybe I should call him. Or I'll stop by at his place this evening.' Captain was focused on strategy for the afternoon. But Javid had this to add '*Saala, us Patkar ka bad luck kharab hain yaar, usne he Naru ko panvati lagaein hogi*'.

Arjun would never forget the funeral. His crumpled mother propped up by the stoic Savitri Kaki. His father's bloodshot eyes beseeching reason. So many questions. So what had just prevailed?

LUCK? DESTINY? FATE?

If everything is preordained, why even TRY?

Was it Naru's fault?

The flames rose high off the pyre, carried away by a soothing afternoon breeze. The lingering smell was acrid, but familiar. Arjun watched his father. The forlorn and broken figure, a shell now if he had ever been stronger. What was his FAULT? WHY? What use.... ADVERSITY?

A few pieces fell into place in his mind. In that big mental Escheresque jigsaw puzzle. He could not put a finger on them. But answers were forming. And the questions became less insistent.

The next few days passed in a blur. Arjun scored runs at will as his team marched through the inter-school's tournament. He could not be stopped. His individual heroics catapulted the tourney into the headlines. Flattering descriptions of his batting prowess graced the sports pages of all the major dailies. A few carried photographs. His grubby gloves were always in stark contrast to his squeaky clean whites.

The final was anticlimactic. Arjun made it a personal romp as he smashed a double century and then snagged a few wickets with his off spinners. Now completely superstitious and unable to venture onto the cricket field without the gloves, Arjun even took to bowling and fielding with the gloves in his pocket. His family came for the prize distribution, all of them beaming from ear to ear as first Pranay climbed up on the podium to receive the shield and then Arjun, a tall gleaming trophy for the 'man of the tournament'. The next morning his father glanced briefly at the headlines before turning to the sports page. His heart swelled with pride to see a smiling Arjun holding aloft his trophy. Putting the paper down he turned to his wife, 'I must say I am surprised. That good for nothing loafer finally got his act together to excel at something.'

Just then Arjun sleepily entered the room.

'Here is the great Gary Sobers himself.' His father continued.

Allowing himself a leisurely stretch Arjun replied, 'Baba, he was left handed, and I don't really bowl.'

Mr. Athavale looked up sharply at his son, deciding that some bubble bursting was called for. '*Hanh*. Otherwise the comparison is justified? *Arre*, hero! Get your head out of the clouds. Time to hit the books. Otherwise the finals will hit you for a six.'

Preempting a flare up, Mrs. Athavale chimed in with a truculent, 'Let him be. He has just woken up!'

'About time.' Mr. Athavale grunted.

Cricket still on his mind, Arjun said, 'Baba, I'll probably get called up for the Bombay schools team.'

Unable to keep the pride entirely out of his voice, Mr. Athavale cautioned, 'Talk to your teachers about it. Maybe Dabholkar sir can arrange for some one on one instruction. I don't want your studies to suffer. You musn't close any doors, develop all of your abilities, give your potential its due. This cricket will not last you a lifetime. What happens after that? What if you don't make it? Your forefathers haven't left you any diamond mines.

You are going to need a career or a trade; otherwise you'll end up in some clerical job… or worse. Take it from me; life is not fun at the bottom of the food chain.'

Sensing another need for situation defusement, Mrs. Athavale bustled over to the table with hot *parathas*.

'*Puray, Puray*! Enough already. You are all going to get indigestion.' Turning to her husband she promised, 'I will go to his school today.'

Gathering up his things with a hurried look at his wristwatch, Mr. Athavale stepped into his shoes and turned around to Arjun, 'All right then, I am off. Coming Bachcha?'

His mouth full of hot *paratha*, Arjun waved his father on, 'In a bit *baba*. You go ahead.' Watching his father's retreating back, Arjun turned slowly to his mother, 'Why is he never happy? I got the inter-schools 'man of the tournament' award. Isn't that good enough for him?'

Accustomed to providing pacifying translation between father and son, his mother mollified him. 'You think he isn't happy? You can't see it? He is immensely happy and proud of you! He only wants the best for you. All of this is for you both, the children. You think he cares about himself?'

She paused and looked up at the smiling picture of her oldest child, the twinkle in his eyes not apparent through the reflective glass. A heavy garland of marigolds obscured a large part of his face.

'Naru,' she sighed, paused.

Unable to continue, the words choked in a ball at the bottom of her throat and tears readily squirted out. She regained her composure and quickly wiped her moist eyes with the end of her sari.

'We agonize over so many things, wondering what effect they will have on your future. If you do well, our life is a success. All the time we parents put away our own ambitions and needs, and look to invest in your future; our children. We want to empower you to do your best and it hurts when you don't. But enough of that…eat up and get ready or you will be late. Don't forget to take your *dabba*.'

Arjun pushed back his chair, grabbed a last piece of *paratha*. He followed his mother's gaze to his brother's photograph and sighed, '*Achha Aai*, All right then!'

2

A few days later as Arjun walked towards Dadar station with his kitbag slung over his shoulder, a creased brow tacitly revealed that he was engrossed in apparent intense cerebration. He sauntered by Pranay without noticing him. The evening bustle was still a few hours away. Pranay called out to him and warily crossed the street, adeptly bypassing a motorcyclist and a vegetable vendor to join his friend. Slapping him on his back he asked, 'Arjun how are the Bombay schools nets?'

Arjun looked up brightly. 'Good!' a shadow of guilt crossed his face. 'You should be there. You are a much better cricketer than I. I feel like a fraud, being there, just because of the gloves...,' he continued.Pranay stepped back and looked Arjun squarely in the eye, 'There you go again with that bogus gloves talk. Gloves don't bat, you do, and you better start believing that. Something just went off, to uncork you, let out the fizz, you know like a Coke bottle.' Not quite convinced Arjun shook his head, 'Coke bottle! Listen to you! You are too much.' 'What are your plans after the national tourney?' Pranay continued conversationally.'Back to the books, I think. I must say I am not looking forward to it.' Arjun replied as they passed a newsstand. The evening editions were prominently displayed in front, while garish film magazines competed with sport publications in the back. Pranay walked over and picked up the evening paper. He glanced down and immediately looked up, his eyes shining. He let out a loud whoop and said enigmatically, 'I don't think you are going to play the nationals.'Startled, Arjun's gaze shifted from Pranay to the newspaper in his hand, 'What! What are you...,' he started. But Pranay's eyes twinkled, he was on a roll, 'And forget about those books for a bit.' Arjun lunged for the paper as Pranay stepped aside nimbly. With his hands on his hips Arjun queried,

'Have you gone nuts? What are you...?' Pranay thrust the paper toward Arjun. 'You have been called up to play for the Mumbai Ranji trophy team. It says here that you are expected to join the nets tomorrow.' Arjun grabbed the paper, 'Get outta here! Show me that.'

At that very moment, Mr. Athavale walked into his flat. An early departure from his office had afforded him some extra time at 'Casbah'. Time, in his view, well spent. The evening edition that he had scanned while nursing his drink had lifted his sprits further. *Joie de vivre* writ large upon his face, he waved the newspaper in his hand vigorously; not unlike a weary traveler beckoning a familiar face after a long train journey. Seeing nobody around, he threw the paper down and rushed into the room shouting;

'Anybody home? Pallavi, Arjun.'

Both Pallavi and her mother rushed out. The excited tone conveyed the fact that there was news that needed to be shared; pronto.

'Where is Arjun?' he looked around, unwilling to begin without the entire potential audience.

Arjun charged in through the open flat door beaming. He had been running. 'Here I am,' he panted.

Trying to bring some order to the proceedings his mother asked, 'What happened? What's the excitement?' Turning to her and grabbing the newspaper for another excited wave, Anand Athavale beamed.

'Haven't you heard?' The suspense was overwhelming.

Pallavi grabbed the newspaper and demanded an explanation, 'No we haven't. Now will someone tell us please?'

Mr. Athavale grabbed the newspaper back and with another emphatic wave he announced, 'Arjun has been called for the Mumbai team nets.'

His eyes moistened as he turned to his smiling son. Putting a hand on his shoulder he looked his son in the eye; his eyes straying momentarily to Naru gazing down from the wall.

'Guess I was wrong. You proved me wrong Bachcha. You can make something of your potential.' Unwilling to accept praise that he felt was clearly undeserved, Arjun attempted to clarify.

'That's not really it. It's not...'

Pallavi had been containing her rising excitement but could give politeness it's due no longer, 'Ranji trophy!!! Arjun you aren't even 15. Most of those bowlers bowl 6 times faster than your age, and that's in miles per hour. You aren't even tall enough to deal with those bowlers, the ball is going to come to you from a higher altitude, take a different trajectory. The vector forces of your strokes will be all wrong. You are going to have to modify your backlift.'

Appropriately miffed, Arjun snorted, 'Thanks for your vote of confidence!'

The excitement abating; his father inquired, 'What about your exams?'

Arjun turned to him. 'Whoa there, hold your horses. I have just been called for nets. That too, not officially. I may not even get selected! They haven't contacted us yet.'

Jolted out of her thoughts Mrs. Athavale interjected, 'Who is they? Some singhji...ram called..'

'EEEk, Ram Singh Kullarpur!' Pallavi shrieked.

'From CBA, I think?' Mrs. Athavale continued.

'BCA' Arjun clarified.

'Bombay Cricket Association,' Mr. Athavale explained to his wife.

'He said he would call later..' Mrs. Athavale wanted to finish, when the shrill ring of the telephone curtly interrupted the verbal exchange.

The family turned towards the instrument in unison. First to recover, Pallavi ran and picked up the phone. She spoke animatedly into it and then beckoned Arjun. The family gathered around Arjun as he spoke, alternately waving to his family to give him room and covering his free ear in an endeavor to concentrate on the voice at the other end. He put the phone down, turned smiling, 'I'm in,' he declared, pumping his fists, his characteristic demonstration of elation.

What about GOOD fortune? Is that ever undeserved? Do we even question it? How should one deal with it? With Equanimity? Probe for an explicit EXPLANATION? How ROBUST is it? How TRANSIENT?

Happy recollections formed a cineloop and gusted through Arjun's mind as he tried to sleep. Is this EUPHORIA? He liked it. Why is EUPHORIA or even HAPPINESS not permanent?

The sweet gooey taste of Savitri kaki's besan laddoos. His parents joy when Pallavi won the middle school scholarship. That sweet sound when he timed a shot perfectly.

HAPPINESS formed a web whose filigree seeped into his brain. MOMENTS and MEMORIES that had become more beautiful and less real with time.

GOOD FORTUNE did not need to make sense because it was..... GOOD FORTUNE!

3

Arjun hurried home after school the next evening. He gulped down his milk and rushed into his room to pack up his kit. His first day at the Mumbai nets; apprehension bubbled like boiling oil around *jalebis*. Unable to readily locate some things he looked around first methodically then frantically, rummaging through his clothes. He emptied his drawers onto the floor scattering his clothes around. His mother entered the room looking mysteriously sly, if Arjun had cared to notice.

'Looking for something?' she inquired lightheartedly.

Arjun missed the flippancy in her voice. Without looking up, he replied, 'I can't find my kit. I had left it here. Now the entire bag is gone.'

'Are you talking about that stinky duffel bag?' continued his mother good-humouredly.

Anxious to locate the misplaced bag, Arjun concurred. 'Yeah! That's the one. Have you seen it?'

'No, but I have a surprise for you.' She stepped out of the room and returned with a spanking new white kit bag with the fashionable Nike swoosh adorning its side and handed it over to a bewildered Arjun.

His voice rising in a panicky crescendo Arjun stated the obvious, 'That isn't mine. Where is my bag?' he asked looking around, hopeful that the truant piece of luggage would mysteriously materialize.

'Your father took some time off from work today and bought you these.' Mrs. Athavale explained as she dramatically opened the zipper of the new bag. 'Look, new trousers, shirt and gloves. And you thought he was never

44

pleased, that he did not appreciate you!'

Now on the verge of hysteria Arjun urgently asked, 'Where is my old kit?'

Puzzled by her son's lack of excitement at what seemed to be an appropriate and somewhat extravagant gift; his mother clarified, 'I think he gave it to the *raddiwala*, right next to the sports store, near the station. But what....'

Without waiting for his mother to finish, Arjun rushed to the front door, turning around to explain. 'You don't understand it's not me, I can't, .. not without...' he bumped into his father at the door and couldn't hold back a mordant, 'Thanks *baba*!', on his way out.

Mr. Athavale managed a hesitant 'Welcome!' as his son rushed by. He turned to his wife and inquired, 'What now?' he looked at the kit. 'He didn't like it?'

His confused wife could only shrug.

Arjun charged into the sports store, breathless. Without pausing to catch his breath he demanded the manager's attention. Recognizing him from the numerous times that Arjun had visited the store in the past the manager smiled indulgently. He motioned to Arjun to slow down and gave him his full attention.

'The *raddiwala*,' Arjun started.

'What about him?' The puzzled manager asked.

'Where is he?' I need to get my gloves!' Arjun continued urgently.

'Next door, but what happened to the new ones your father picked up yesterday? Did you lose them already?'

Arjun was in a hurry to get to the *raddiwala*. 'Those are no good!' he shouted back by way of explanation, as he rushed into the ramshackle store next door. The young man supervising the purchase of old newspapers in the front of the store remembered the old kit bag and gloves. He also recollected selling them off almost immediately.

'To whom? Please think. I must have them.' Arjun pleaded. The young man gave it a brief thought but his memory failed him and he turned away. The other customers at the store clamored for his attention.

Arjun returned home dejectedly and walked by his parents with a morose mug. He refused to answer their questioning looks. He picked up his spanking white new kitbag, packed in his new stuff and walked out of the door leaving his bewildered parents staring at each other.

The evening sun cast a warm glow on the lush green cricket field. The racket of the bustling city seemed far away. Nets were just getting underway and a throng of players were desultorily stretching. Arjun walked up to the gathering unsure of whom to approach. His arrival prompted little excitement. A few players directed inquiring looks at him and each other. An older gentleman broke away from the throng and approached him.

'Arjun is it? Welcome. Changing rooms over there. Join the warm ups. By the way, I am the coach.'

Visibly overwhelmed, Arjun sputtered, 'Okay Mr. Bandhu, I mean I know... I recognized..'

Smiling the coach turned to him; 'Call me coach.' Arjun walked away, laid his kit down and hesitantly joined the other players stretching. After a few moments the players ran to the end of the field and back, breaking into a sprint at the urging of their coach. The coach addressed them, divided them into groups and initiated some fielding practice. Arjun was assigned to a group taking close in catching practice. Butterflies in his tummy made Arjun nervously floor the first few.

The coach walked over to him, 'I was even more nervous on my first day,' he reassured. He cupped his hands together and demonstrated, 'Try to see the ball into your hands.' Arjun held onto the next few, the coach turned his attention to the nets. The first batsman had padded up and was walking in. The bowlers marked their run-ups and waited for the batsman to settle in. Arjun stood hesitantly in the outfield. The coach caught his eye and gestured him to stand at mid on. Adarkar, having had some international experience was the marquee bowler on display. Waiting for his turn to bowl he turned to his teammate.

'Who's the new kid?'

'Arjun something! Had a great run in the inter schools,' the teammate volunteered solemnly.

Sizing up the new kid, Adarkar seemed unimpressed. 'Straight from schools eh!'

Precisely at that moment, Arjun stood nervously at mid-on. The higher level of cricket was not as intimidating as the loss of his talismanic gloves. He found it difficult to concentrate and kept his fingers crossed hoping against hope that he would not be asked to bat. The separation from the apparently magical gloves had sapped his confidence. The regulars in the

Mumbai side padded up in succession and took their turn at the batting crease. The setting sun threatened to dip behind the huge concrete facade of the stadium when the coach turned to Arjun and gestured to him to pad up. Arjun tried to look away but could not ignore his gesticulating coach for long. Reluctantly he padded up, slid in a guard into his jockstrap and walked in to bat. The bowlers waited till he was ready. One of them turned to Adarkar.

'Anil! *Naya bakra hai. Hila ke rakh de!*'

Adarkar smiled and ambled in to bowl, his first ball was slightly short. Arjun couldn't judge the bounce and was hit on the shoulder. Adarkar next hit him on the helmet as he awkwardly tried to duck and finally in his gut, causing Arjun to double up in pain. The coach called for the ball from Adarkar and tossed it to the left arm spinner. Adarkar walked away to get a drink while Arjun confronted the guiles of the lefty. He did not make contact with the first three balls he faced and then was bowled on three consecutive deliveries as he heaved in futility at the ball.

'Welcome to the big league,' Adarkar shouted as the coach asked Arjun to step down. The next batsman took his place.

That evening Arjun returned home disconsolately. Pallavi ran out to meet him. Her eager questions were met with a stony silence. Arjun looked up at her and tears welled up in his eyes. She backed away as he strode by her into his room. Later at dinner, his father even related a few funny anecdotes about Mr. Cawasji, a co-worker, to cheer him up. Arjun looked down at his plate unwaveringly, disappearing into his room as soon as he was done.

He lay in bed staring at the ceiling his stony face betraying no emotion, providing no clue about his thoughts. He heard a sound outside his room and in no mood for any further attempts at conversation, snapped his eyes shut. His mother walked in. A quick look at his face revealed that he was obviously feigning sleep. She ran her hand through his hair, lingering over the last few strands. Her eyes were drawn to an angry purple bruise on his shoulder. She reached to touch it. Arjun winced, and his mother drew away with sharp intake of her breath. She walked out of the room and returned with some oil which she slowly rubbed on to the shoulder. The soothing rhythmic motion cleared the furrows on Arjun's brow as he drifted into a restless, dreamless sleep.

Nets the next day were more exasperating if that was possible. Arjun could not get into any rhythm; his failures prompting reckless stroke-play. Despite the instructions, cajoling and eventual pleading by the coach Arjun was unable to display any batting prowess. The Coach was obviously frustrated and shared his feelings with some of the other officials around. Disconsolate, Arjun could barely fight back tears as he packed up and walked to the station. The harsh neon lights on the platform highlighted his tear-streaked cheeks. A few in the bustling crowd around him paused to stare more closely. Arjun averted his eyes from their kind, inquiring looks. He stood at the doorway in the local train despite being cautioned by his mother not to do so, allowing the humid air to dry the tears on his cheeks.

As he trudged home, depressed and demoralized, Pranay caught up with him. Sensing his friend's mood, he laid a hand on his shoulder and with forced cheerfulness asked, 'Hey! Where have you been? Or does the Ranji player not need his old friends. I came looking for you yesterday, but your mother said you were already asleep.'

Without looking up, Arjun mumbled, 'I lost them!'

The essence of what was being said still unclear, Pranay continued, 'Lost what! Your marbles?' Pranay parlayed a nervous laugh.

Arjun looked up and glared at his friend, 'The gloves, Pranay. THE GLOVES. My dad threw them out,' he snapped.

Shocked, Pranay replied, 'HE DID WHAT?' Taken aback by his own panic Pranay feigned candor and quickly continued. 'Anyway, I never bought the baloney about the gloves.'

Not quite ready to cheer up, Arjun lapsed into a mumble. 'I don't have it any more. I am horrible at the nets. Even the coach is incensed. I don't think I am going back tomorrow.'

Looking at his friend directly Pranay implored. 'Don't do that. It's probably just nerves. Hang in there. You know what most of us would give for...'

He stopped short as Arjun looked up. Both boys were painfully aware that all Pranay ever wanted was the opportunity that Arjun had. Shaking his head, confused by the swirling chaos of self-pity and guilt in his mind, Arjun stepped away and crossed the road. He turned back to tearfully say, 'I don't want to talk about it.'

Pranay shouted after the retreating figure, 'Don't make hasty decisions. Sleep on it. Sleep late, it's Sunday. I will talk to you tomorrow.'

Arjun didn't look back. Pranay waited a moment then shrugged and turned away.

MISFORTUNE, another meaningless crime. It was hard to accept. Hard not to ask why? WHY me? WHY now?

WORRY and WHAT IFS creased Arjun's brow. He caught himself in the mirror and recoiled. His scrunched up face looked just like Savitri kaki's leathery one. Existential ANGST did that?

What use was a WHAT IF?

Unless. Unless one built on it. Gleaned a nugget of positivity out of a mound of negativity.

LIFE is not a parable.

The next day Arjun maintained a laconic exterior, rebuffing any attempts at conversation. His family, by now accustomed to his mood swings left him well alone. After a sumptious breakfast of steaming *idlis* garnished with oil and crunchy *molagapudi*, Arjun set out and his meaningless meandering brought him to a playground. Many of the neighborhood kids were engaged in impromptu games of cricket and a few flew kites braving the criss-crossing games. The chaotic mingling blurred the demarcations between games and the paucity of space usually meant, that mid-on in one game was actually in the slip cordon of another, although facing the wrong way. Arjun took a seat and idly looked around. The activity in front of him proceeded at a frenetic pace. Kids darted around, running across other games.

Suddenly his eyes were drawn to a pile of ten rupee notes. They were lying in the grass about twenty feet from him. Fluttering in the wind, a pair of gloves was positioned on them preventing them from taking flight. Not just any pair of gloves, HIS pair. Incredulous, he walked then ran towards a disheveled kid who appeared to be in charge.

'Hey, hey you. Where did you get these?' he asked, pointing to the gloves. Turning to confront his interrogator, the boy who others around him called Pakya suspiciously asked, 'Why?'

Adopting a more appeasing tone, Arjun proceeded to explain, 'They are mine. My father threw them out by mistake.' Nonplussed, Pakya matter-of-factly stated.

'Too bad! They are mine now.'

Rising panic betrayed by the rapidly escalating pitch of his voice, Arjun beseeched. 'Please, I really must have them. I'll give you twenty rupees for them!' The monetary offering piqued Pakya's interest.

'Twenty rupees! I wish I could, but they are part of our bet match, twenty overs a side, that's the pot.' He pointed to the pile of notes. 'Winner takes all.' With a sudden burst of inspiration and enthusiasm Arjun asked, 'Then let me play for you. You won't regret it. Just let me bat with my gloves. I guarantee that we will win.'

The opposing captain walked over just then with a confident swagger and a 'cat that swallowed the canary' kind of expression. 'Hey Pakya! We want to make one change in our team. This guy will just bowl four overs. The last four. Won't bat or field.'

Now vexed with the continued twists to what had started out being a straightforward Sunday morning game, Pakya queried, 'Who?'

Rahim stepped out from behind a group of boys. Pakya gulped, 'Rahim!' Arjun positioned himself next to Pakya, elbowing others to insinuate his mouth next to Pakya's ear. He looked at Rahim sneering across at them and whispered.

'Don't worry. Say Ok. But you would like a change too. That I will bat.' Pakya stepped away and discussed the new development with his teammates, with occasional input from Arjun. Finally he turned around, contorted his face into his best impression of a brave expression and laid down his conditions.

'All right then! But we want to make a change, bring in one batsman. He won't bowl or field. Just bat.' He pointed to Arjun. Now it was the turn of the other team to form a huddle, discuss animatedly, interspersed with Rahim yelling, '*Saala, Pavaskar ko bhi lene de! Chutti kar doonga!*' Finally the cluster broke. The other captain approached Pakya, 'Agreed. But he can bat only in the last four overs.'

Arjun eyed the gloves and urged, 'Say ok!'

Anxious to get the game underway Pakya acquiesced, hissing to Arjun, 'You had better be right. I don't care about the stinky gloves but there is money involved.'

He walked out officiously with the other captain to toss. Arjun looked for a suitable place to sit. Rahim walked by, 'Let's see what you can do in four overs.' Turning back, he added, 'If you last that long!'

The game began. The other team batted first. A young kid, hanging around hoping to be some part of the action was entrusted with the task of scrawling a running score on an old blackboard propped up on a rusty tin. Arjun, with his specialized designation as an exclusive batsman, didn't field but settled down to watch the game. He rubbed his hands together nervously, crestfallen if the other team scored too freely and cheering every wicket with whoops of encouragement.

The other team made 103 in the designated 20 overs. Arjun's team took their turn at the crease. Pakya and another boy opened the innings, and quickly make 74 without loss in 13 overs. Arjun's expression progressed from one of apprehension to one that smelt imminent victory. He divided his attention between the game and directing longing glances at the gloves. Rahim came onto bowl in the 14th over and immediately made an impact, uprooting Pakya's middle stump with his first ball and proceeded to take two more wickets in that over and three more in the 16th. The score read 78 for 6 at the beginning of the 18th over, but not for long as Rahim struck with his first ball again.

Arjun approached Pakya and begged to be sent in to bat. 'Pakya, Rahim, their extra player is changing the game. Why don't you use me?'

Pakya appeared perplexed, 'Hey, I can't do that.' He gestured towards the money. 'The others have paid money to play. How can I ask one of these guys who have fielded, not to bat?'

'But, that was our plan', pleaded Arjun as the hollow sound of leather meeting timber signaled the fall of another wicket. Arjun looked away from Pakya to his other teammates, stridently and urgently imploring, 'Do you want to lose?' Not quite enthralled by the prospect of defeat and the attendant monetary loss the remaining batsmen nodded. Arjun jumped up and grabbed the gloves. He hastily fastened a pad onto his left leg and rushed in to bat. Rahim had two more balls left in his third over and bowled his in-swinging yorkers; the deliveries that had befuddled the preceding batsmen and got him all his wickets. Arjun was untroubled and stepped forward, dispatching both to the cover fence.

The kid writing the scoreboard had a little trouble with his rapid addition and quickly consulted his friends before arduously scribbling 86 for 8. The nineteenth over had number 10 struggling with the first three balls as the fielders crowded him. He finally managed to edge the fourth for a single. Arjun helped himself to 4 of the 5th and glanced the last ball to fine leg and crossed over to keep strike. The ball decelerated as it approached Rahim on the fine leg fence. In a burst of inspiration Rahim kicked the ball over the boundary line; signaling a four and forced Arjun away from the strike.

As Rahim walked back to commence the last over, nine runs were needed. There was a brief break in the action as a loose kite, with it's string trailing wafted across the playing field, pursued by a swarm of urchins brandishing sticks and shouting 'Caughtela hai', to establish possession of the multi-colored kite. Order was restored, but not before the kite was ripped by two warring imps. Rahim loosened up and came charging in. The first ball whizzed by the tail-ender missing bat and stumps by a hair. On the next, the batsman was not that lucky as an ungainly heave left middle stump in the horizontal position. The last man walked in to bat and flinched as the third ball flew by before he could move out of his stance. He then proceeded to demonstrate the handsome drive that he had planned to play before settling down to face the fourth ball. Again beaten by sheer speed, the last man scrambled gratefully to the non-strikers end as the ball ricocheted off his front pad.

Calmly, Arjun surveyed the field before crouching into his stance. Rahim delivered a gorgeous out-swinger pitching up and leaving the batsman late. Arjun dabbed at it; his fine edge just eluded the outstretched right hand of the wicketkeeper as the ball sped to the fence.

With the last ball coming up and four runs required for a win, Rahim sent all of his fielders including the wicket keeper to the boundary. Arjun stepped back and looked around to see ten fielders on the fence. Rahim looked at him and grinned, 'Not this time! Not again.'

Rahim dug the last ball in short and seeing Arjun move to make room on the leg side, he directed it further outside the off stump at the last minute. Arjun had no option but to flail at it. The ball ballooned off the top edge skying towards third man. 'Stay back, stay back and stop the four,' Rahim shouted. The ball billowed up invitingly. Years of programmed learning, that balls like these should be caught and the possibility of clinching victory for his side whilst ensuring a personal blaze of glory propelled third man forward. Rahim shouted for him to go back. The confused fielder lurched off the fence towards the now dipping ball. Rahim's screamed admonishments caused him to hesitate as the ball now enamored with gravity hurtled down and thudded onto the ground. The spin imparted by the vicious slice in the stroke made it swerve away from a now distraught third man. The kid who saw himself carried away on his teammates shoulders a few moments before, turned to see the innocent looking ball trickle over the fence. Seeing an enraged Rahim fuming towards him third man hastened along the path taken by the ball. He did not stop to pick it up and jumped over the nearest fence to escape Rahim's justified wrath.

Pakya and his friends were overjoyed and took turns to hug Arjun. Their attention quickly turned to the division of the spoils. Arjun quietly picked up the gloves which Pakya parted with, with some reluctance. Finally with a wink to Pakya that said both thank you and goodbye, Arjun walked away.

Arjun arrived at the nets that evening with a hitherto unseen confidence. Most of his teammates acknowledged him with more than a nod and less than a full fledged welcoming smile, a sort of shrug-grin. He ran around crisply and fielded well, throwing himself around to grab balls. He made some stellar catches and stops in the field. Finally the coach asked him to bat.

Arjun padded up quickly, finally pulling out his gloves. The teammate who had egged Adarkar to embarrass him the previous days was fielding at short midwicket. Seeing the soiled gloves he yelled, 'Hey! What's with the gloves? Mama stitch them at home or did dad make his first runs with them.' The others at the nets laughed at this witticism and even the taciturn coach cracked a smile.

'In 1950,' he added, provoking a fresh round of laughter.

Encouraged, midwicket turned back and shouted, *'Arre Anil aa gaya bakra, hila ke rakh de!'*

Arjun took his stance as Adarkar ambled in to bowl to him. Arjun was content to dab defensively at the other bowlers but struck Adarkar furiously; unleashing a delectable array of strokes. The coach covered his smiling face and settled to watch the duel as Adarkar increased his run up, bent his back and even no-balled to extract greater pace. All to no avail as Arjun imperiously continued his rakish dismemberment of Adarkar's bowling.

4

The bobbling egg yolk like sun, framed by a cottony cumulous cloud, slithered towards the ground as the evening shadows lengthened on the balcony of the pavilion. Five gentlemen sat on the verandah enjoying their evening tea. The worries of the world seemed to lie squarely on their shoulders. One of them, fingering his trademark bowtie nervously verbalized their feelings, 'Shitty time to be a selector. All these injuries and the Challenger trophy coming up.'

Attempting to direct the conversation towards specifics a second gentleman remarked, 'We all know that Suchen, Nakul and Gourav can bat. We should be trying to sift through the others. We probably have the most youngsters in the world playing the game. With such a surfeit of talent there should be more diamonds in the rough.'

A half-eaten *bhajiya* poised in midair the third national selector added, 'The gap between them and the others seems to be getting wider.' The *bhajiya* finally made it into the cavernous mouth. Not quite done with his monologue the first selector tried to wrest back the dialogue.

'Hey, that's not fair. What about Bharath, Jugraj, Hiru and Saif?'

The second selector beamed and banged his fist down to emphasize, 'That's just what I am talking about. If you are so sold on the guys we already have, how are you going to judge new talent? If we look at the Indian national side as an enclave of a privileged few, we are going to miss out on some great young talent. All because of *status quo* blinders and the great black hole of inertia.' He finished dramatically with an admonishing wave of his hand.

Seeing that there was no opportunity to deliver his own monologue the first selector turned away. The repeated sound of willow belting leather drew his attention.

'Hey, who's this kid?'

Glad to enter the conversation now that the *bhajiyas* were all gone the diminutive fourth gentleman reported. 'Some wunderkind who did well in the schools tourney. Actually won it single-handedly for his school. A bit of a Jekyl and Hyde with the bat. Can range from horrible to sensational. I watched him the last few days, he was atrocious.'

The nervous bowtie stroking now evolved into a more vigorous yanking. The first selector instructed his cohorts, 'Well he is hitting Anil off his length! Stop talking, let's look.'

That evening the aftermath of the sunset endowed a surreal dusky pink tinge to the twilight. Late evening bugs dashed around aimlessly. For a change the humidity dipped and the air was as crisp as a paper *dosa*. Flushed with his exertions and unable to fully contain his obvious pleasure in his own performance, Arjun busied himself packing up. On his way home he rode the train with a new swagger. The cool breeze and evening smells added to the enjoyment of the moment. At dinner his family was pleasantly surprised to behold a loquacious Arjun. The misery that had till the day before encompassed him was now a thing of the past. The family knew better than to look a gift horse in the mouth. They exchanged quizzical looks and accepted the unexplained mood change gladly.

A TV show chronicling the accomplishments of a young actor competed for attention with a hot dinner. The show went to commercials, louder than the hushed tones of the show's anchor. The family rose together. Arjun's mother started cleaning up. Pallavi grabbed a book, his father switched channels and Arjun moved towards his room. The TV was switched on to a news channel and the pretty newscaster was closing with a reprise of the headlines.

'Teenage cricket phenomenon Arjun Athavale has been named to replace the injured VVS Bharath in the upcoming Challenger trophy. Bharath was injured while batting in the nets at Hyderabad. Arjun is a high schooler yet to play his first First-class cricket game. He is touted by many as the best new talent after Suchen Chemburkar.' Arjun stopped in his tracks.

True to form Pallavi let out a loud shriek and was the first to yell, 'Challenger trophy! You are going to play with all the top stars.'

Mrs. Athavale hurried out of the kitchen habitually wiping her hands on her *pallu*. Arjun's father stopped to look up. All eyes were on Arjun. Under such close scrutiny, Arjun appeared a bit flustered. He gazed at his kitbag for reassurance.

'What's up *bachcha*? Aren't you excited? Or are things happening a bit too quickly?' his mother asked. Her voice was laced with concern at her son's apparent lack of enthusiasm.

Arjun sounded confused, unable to decide how he should feel at this sudden upward swing in fortune. 'I don't know if I am going to do well. I had a great day at the nets. I know the selectors were around. I don't know!' Arjun paced the room. His agitation made all the others in the room tense.

'Arjun, here, come here. Sit. *Bachcha*, you must be good, otherwise they would not have picked you.' His father cajoled. 'Now it is your job to go out there and do your best. Have confidence in all your skills, your inner strengths. Give it your all and good things will happen.'

Not fully convinced, Arjun managed to nod and summon up a weak smile, 'Challenger trophy! I'll at least get to see the top players up close,' he remarked facetiously. Pallavi had procured the remote and was surfing through various channels eventually settling on a sports channel that was carrying a commentary by Saumil Pavaskar glibly titled 'Suamy Sez'. Pavaskar filled the screen and began in his customary clipped tone, making a suggestive grabbing gesture.

'Finally the selectors are showing some testicular fortitude. The selection of Arjun Athavale is notable only because we have been seeing the same faces in and out of the national side. There is always a danger of forming close-knit cliques and thus shutting out young talent. I don't expect him to do well. The stage is too big, the stakes too high and the kid is too inexperienced. But I will gladly eat my words with a generous helping of humble pie, if he proves me wrong. The other matter grabbing the attention of the cricketing world this week...'

Before he could elucidate on the other matter, Pallavi turned the TV off and turned beaming to her brother. The news finally did sink in and the happy family sat down to discuss it. The cheery jangle of the phone precluded any constructive conversation as numerous callers offered congratulations and advice. The first match of the Challenger trophy was just a few days away and Arjun spent his time at the Mumbai nets, where he was now treated with increasing respect, daydreaming. The major substance of his dreams centered on a single-handed heroic victory clinching batting performance on his part.

The evening before Arjun turned in early. The pragmatic Pranay had called everyday to remind him that proper rest would ensure a relaxed body and mind and improve the chances of a good outing.

'Mens sana in corpore sano' he offered sagaciously, as if the Latin made the words truer.

The day of the first game dawned cloudy. Menacing turgid clouds hovered in the sky as Arjun made his way to Wankhede stadium. The pavilion was abuzz with activity as Arjun walked in hesitantly and settled in a deep chair in a corner. Players walked about. They all seemed to know each other and shouted pleasantries, as they went about the business of getting ready for the game. As the captains walked out to toss, India's current captain Gourav Rangoli caught sight of Arjun. Asking his opposite number to give him a moment he walked over to him.

'Hi. You must be Arjun. I am your captain. Welcome! Hope you don't mind Arjun. You are 12th man for today's game.'

His mouth agape at being addressed with such familiarity by one of his heroes; all Arjun could manage was an unintelligible burble. His excitement reached a crescendo and he had to suppress a sudden inexplicable urge to take flight. As an afterthought he whipped out a little notebook out of his kit bag and turned to his captain.

'Sir, can I have your autograph please?'

His captain grinned as he walked away, 'Of course! All in good time.' Gourav then added, self-deprecatingly, with a twinkle in his eye; 'Maybe I should take yours now. From what I hear you may be soon replacing me in the India XI.'

Arjun was genuinely shocked. 'No way!' he blurted before he realized that his captain was kidding. Gourav departed with a good natured, 'You just watch kid!'

The game started. His side was fielding first and Arjun took a seat in the front row to watch the proceedings. Their opening bowler sent down a fiery spell and grabbed a few wickets but didn't get adequate support from the other end which hemorrhaged runs freely. The scoreboard moved rapidly. Caught in the carousel of stroke-making, wickets falling, and batsmen walking back and forth, Arjun forgot for a moment that he was a player in the game.

The opening bowler returned to the dressing room for a break after his first spell. Jogged out of his daydream Arjun was called in to field and almost tripped down the steps in his excitement. Recovering, he ran out rapidly and was directed to field on the long-off fence. The ball was hit to almost every other part of the ground in the next few overs. Finally, the batsman hit a lofted straight drive towards him. Butterflies rose like angry hornets in his stomach. He reached out for the ball, fumbled it and conceded a boundary. Four runs. Arjun was deflated; Gourav walked over to him and placed a hand on his shoulder.

'Calm down. We all have first match jitters. Just try to focus away from your nervousness. You okay?' he asked. Arjun shook his head in the affirmative.

After that the ball seemed to follow Arjun and he redeemed himself by making several sharp boundary line saves and capped his efforts by holding onto a well-judged running catch. The pacer returned to field. Arjun left gloomily and got a smattering of nepotistic applause from his hometown cricket savvy Mumbai crowd. The match drew to its close and Arjun's team was victorious.

The tired players returned from the field and the dressing room echoed with 'Good game' and 'Well played'. Arjun was at the receiving end of many a well-meaning back slap. His captain walked over to him, towel slung over a careless shoulder; 'Good show kid! Great team spirit. Keep up the good work.'

Arjun mumbled a hasty thanks and sent one heavenwards for seeing him through his first real test, unscathed.

That evening at the dinner table Arjun was more animated. He monopolized the conversation and the family was keen to hear the details of his exploits. Arjun waxed eloquent pausing briefly every now and then to shovel some food into his mouth.

'..And they are all so nice. I think I improved ten-fold just watching them play. And they all made me feel like I belonged, and you know Dada...'

'Dada?' Pallavi queried.

'Gourav asked me to call him that, yes! He said that I would probably replace him in the national side. Of course, he was just joking.' Arjun continued.

Pushing forward his dinner plate with the contented sigh that could only originate from gastric juices suitably pacified, his mood considerably alleviated by the few quick ones that he had imbibed on his way home, Mr. Athavale turned to his son, 'No games for four days. Might as well put in some time reading. The exams are drawing near. I met Mr. Dabholkar from your school. He said he would be happy to give you some extra math coaching to make-up for what you miss...'

His wife always the voice of reason interrupted, 'The boy is so excited. Will any thought, forget math, ever stick in his head? Arjun where are you going, finish your *poli*.'

Arjun pushed back his chair and charged away from the dining table, 'Just want to talk to Pranay. I will be right back. Great *phulkas* Aai!'

His father was about to protest, he had not quite finished what he wanted to say. But Arjun had bolted leaving the reverberations of the door banging shut in his wake.

That night Arjun pulled out his books and spread them out before him. He started in earnest, scribbling out some math problems on rough sheets of paper. His attempts to concentrate were futile; his mind was filled with the sounds of cricket. A muted crowd roar formed the background, the crack of a full blooded drive and the whiz of a delicate cut beat a staccato rhythm. An excited commentator's voice sang his praises. Arjun finally closed his book recognizing that he wasn't getting anywhere and with a smile on his face, sat back to enjoy his very own symphony.

At the next game Arjun was a little more familiar with the other players. A few slapped him on his back in passing and made polite conversation. Arjun walked to where he sat with the other reserves during the prior game. Spotting him, Gourav tried to attract his attention; finally walking over to talk to him.

'No 3 or no. 6' he asked.

Arjun turned to face his captain, not quite comprehending. 'What?'

'Where would you like to bat?' his captain elucidated.

After a mental pinch to preclude hallucinations Arjun yelped, 'I'm playing?'

Gourav continued his train of thought. 'No. 3 probably. If Jugi plays as well as he did in the last game you may not get a bat.'

The game commenced. Arjun's team fielded first. They began well claiming a few early wickets but a stodgy middle order stemmed the rot. Arjun was adequate in the outfield; not called upon to do anything spectacular. The opposing team finished its quota of overs and the teams returned to the clubhouse for lunch.

Play was about to resume in the afternoon session. Gourav and his opening partner limbered up as the fielding side walked out. Arjun sat aside, the intensity of the moment apparent on his flushed face. Gourav reached into his bag and handed a pair of gloves to Arjun.

'Here kid. My lucky gloves. Got a double hundred on debut with them. Maybe you will get a triple.' With that he smiled and walked out to bat.

The innings began with a flurry of scoring shots on the off side from Gourav. His opening partner was content to push and prod till he had a sudden rush of blood and holed out in the deep.

As he walked back Arjun prepared himself; nervously checked his gear. He lifted his tattered gloves and then looked at the ones his captain had just given him. He was torn; finally reaching a decision he picked up his new gloves and walked out. Gourav met him halfway and walked back to the wicket with him.

'Now take it easy kid,' he advised. 'I know how you feel; been there, done that you know. Take your time to get your eye in. The odd ball is keeping low and the offie has a well-disguised straight one. Don't think too much just get a feel...' They reached the wicket.

Arjun took guard and looked around anxiously. The off spinner trundled in and delivered his slow stuff. Arjun was beaten badly outside the off on the first two balls. He was unable to gauge the length and direction of turn and the ball whipped off the wicket rather quickly. The bowler looked skyward wondering what more he had to do to get a wicket.

The next ball was a half volley. Arjun gleefully cracked it through the covers and Gourav charged down for the run. The fielder at short cover made a great diving stop. As it was his call Arjun contemplated sending his captain back. But seeing him charging in purposefully he feebly ran towards the non- strikers end as the ball was lobbed there for an easy run out. Gourav walked up to him as Arjun walked past him on the way back.

'My fault. It was your call. Why did you do that? They know all about me. They should be seeing you bat,' his captain said.

Arjun paused and then said haltingly. 'You are already set. We can win if you get a big score. It's what's best for the side.'

Gourav watched Arjun's retreating back, impressed by the maturity of one so young; with so much to prove and so much at stake. The game continued; turning into a nail-biting affair. Eventually Gourav got the winning runs in the last over and entered the dressing room tired and happy. After accepting the kudos and congratulations he walked over to Arjun, shook his hand and hugged him. Words were superfluous. At that moment the television commentator was summarizing the game with his closing remarks.

'The biggest disappointment today was the run out of Mumbai's young star Arjun Athavale. He sacrificed his wicket to keep his in-form skipper at the crease. The result was a win for the India 'A' side. Without scoring a run the youngster has served notice and stressed an important fact. One that has eluded the narcissistic, preoccupied minds of today's cricketers. Team comes first. Wins will only be achieved if everyone buys into this philosophy. It certainly augers well for the country's future that one of it's rising stars has already bought into the philosophy that the key to a consistently successful Indian side is maturity and team spirit.'

Arjun returned home to find the house quiet. Pallavi was curled up on the sofa reading. Seeing him walk in she uncoiled and unloaded.

'What were you thinking? You hit the ball at least 160kmph to the throwing hand of a brilliant fielder. He barely had to move. How did you figure you could run 22 yards before the ball got to the non-strikers?'

Not quite in the mood for doses of hard-hitting home-truths; Arjun raised his hand to stem the flow of words from his sister's mouth. 'Pallavi please! I blew it, didn't I. It was not meant to happen. Anybody would kill for the opportunity I had. But Dada was set and playing unbelievably.'

Just then Pranay walked in, 'Good show today Arjun. Not too many out there that would take one for the team.' The two friends stepped out into the balcony.

Arjun obviously had something on his mind, 'You know I didn't bat with them,' he began. 'I did not bat with Suchen's gloves. Dada wanted me to use his. One more chance, that's all I want, one more chance.'

Pranay half-heartedly said, 'It was a run out; surely you don't think the gloves...' and stopped short. Both Pranay and Arjun looked at the kitbag and the gloves sticking out of them. They looked innocuous enough but their perceived powers had enraptured the two young minds.

The day of the final game came all too soon. Arjun walked into the pavilion and was greeted with gusto by the commentators, umpires and other players. Arjun seemed all the more comfortable in his surroundings and was inwardly cringing at the thought that this might be it. That he would not be privy to this place, these people and this familiarity in the future. Gourav greeted him, eyeing his slick white shoes.

'What, new shoes! Did you stop at the temple on your way? Jokes aside, today's your day, show them all you got.'

Nonplussed Arjun croaked, 'Am I in the XI?' The question had occupied his existence for the past few days. Now it was out there, out in the open.

'What did you think? I'd get you run out and then drop you?' Gourav replied casually, as he walked out to toss.

The other team batted first. On a perfect day for cricket, on a featherbed of a wicket the batsmen made merry. The scoreboard rattled along; the carefree atmosphere did eventually get to the batting side. They lost a series of wickets in rapid succession. Finally the innings concluded with a flurry of big hits. Arjun capped a great day in the field with a blinder of a catch half-way to the square leg boundary. The players retreated to the pavilion for lunch. The teams mingled freely, familiar chatter amongst players who had met up after a bit. There were inquiries about families and business ventures, some good natured leg-pulling and ribaldry. Arjun joined in now feeling more a part of the scene. He remembered wondering if he had ever been happier; then reminded himself not to stuff himself with the delicious steaming *pulav*.

Their innings started. Gourav and his opening partner walked out to bat. The first ball was a beauty. A slow inswinger that pitched outside the off stump. Gourav's opening partner shouldered arms quite stylishly only to look back and see his off stump cartwheeling rather elegantly to the wicketkeeper who pouched it with great delight. Arjun struggled into his gear quickly. He looked at his gloves and without a second thought picked up the old tattered ones and walked out confidently. Gourav and Arjun scored freely. The fierce afternoon sun only enhanced their concentration and the fielders' fatigue, as they repeatedly retrieved the ball from the fence. Immaculate stroke-play, precise timing and an occasional savage heave made the scoreboard advance speedily. Both batsmen got fifties in the same over and swiftly moved into their nineties.

The outcome of the game was foregone. Yet the crowd at the stadium sat glued to their seats, mesmerized by the near perfect display of batting. A delectable square cut from Gourav saw him move to 98 with only 4 runs needed to win. The next ball was a full toss from the frustrated spinner. Instinctively Gourav shaped to hit it. A boundary, victory for his side and a ton for him assured. At the very last moment he awkwardly jabbed it away for a single. He then settled down at the non-strikers to watch. Arjun was on strike. The exhilaration of the moment apparent; he heaved at and missed the first ball. The wicketkeeper whipped off the bails.

Arjun was crestfallen as the umpire hesitated and then relieved as the umpire shook his head; 'NOT OUT.'

Without much ado, Arjun dispatched the next ball to the mid wicket boundary, clinching an easy victory for his side. Gourav rushed over to him and patted him on the back. At the pavilion steps the fielders held back and allowed the batsmen to walk ahead. Gourav stopped too and gestured to Arjun to lead the sides in. Wiping sweat that was now mixed with tears Arjun raised his bat to the crowds. Rabi Mantri the ex-India captain now a television commentator stood just outside the dressing room. Arjun was mobbed by the other players. Mantri caught up with Gourav and motioned towards the camera.

'What a game! Full of great shots and classy moments. First let me call up the winning skipper.' Gourav walked up and accepted the trophy. 'Congratulations Dada! Great victory. And a great innings personally. Did you think this was going to be so easy?'

Gourav cleared his throat. 'No, the other team did well. Arjun made it look easy.'

Looking back at the camera Mantri continued; 'Classy gesture on your part, letting the lad get his hundred and the winning runs.'

Unwilling to steal any thunder Gourav graciously said; 'I did nothing. That kid is good.'

'It isn't usual for you to play second fiddle.' Mantri persisted.

Gourav stroked his chin and gave this some thought. 'Like someone wise once said. It was what was best for the team.' His own final words brought a smile to his face as he walked back to his jubilant teammates.

Mantri faced the camera again. 'And now the man of the match. Come on up Arjun.' Unsure and uncertain Arjun walked up sheepishly. In a gesture of feigned familiarity Mantri put his hands on Arjun's shoulder. 'Congratulations! A very mature innings by one so young.'

A pause and the camera panning over to him was a cue for Arjun to respond.

'I am so honoured, what can I say?' Not gifted with the ability to expound endlessly Arjun glared at the camera. Confronted by his inability to come up with coherent speech he walked away gauchely wiping tears that had sprung into his eyes. His teammates hugged him ruffling his hair jovially. Arjun belonged; he felt the pride and joy well up inside him. Sensing the need for solitude during this special moment his teammates walked away.

That evening the conversation was loud at the dinner table. Pallavi excitedly recounted details of Arjun's innings getting up often to demonstrate the strokes played. Arjun looked at her with indulgence occasionally turning to Pranay who had invited himself over and sharing a laugh.

Anand Athavale walked in fresh from an evening bath and his prayers and took his place at the table. His arrival created a temporary lull in the proceedings. He gregariously filled the void.

'I hope there is a videotape of the game available. I heard I missed something special.' He bestowed a glowing affectionate look upon his son. Arjun fidgeted uncomfortably, unused to being the cynosure of all eyes.

Sensing her son's uneasiness his mother got up briskly. 'Now eat up everybody. Arjun, one more *poli*? How about you Pallu? Finish up Arjun get to bed soon, you must be tired. Pallu *raja*, can you help me clean up?'

Arjun and Pranay pushed their chairs back, asked to be excused and stepped out into the verandah. Pranay was anxious to hear some inside, finer details of the game. Arjun was glad to oblige. Pallavi thought about joining them, but hearing her brother's animated narrative sensed that he might prefer to regale Pranay alone. She settled down with a book. An air of well being prevailed in the house which continued into the next morning.

Breakfast had been cleared and the family gathered around the television with a second cup of hot steaming Madras filter coffee; a Sunday morning tradition. Arjun flipped through the channels and again chanced upon Saumil Pavaskar's talk show 'Suamy Sez'. The always garrulous and once prolific ex-India opening batsman was giving his spin on recent happenings and non-happenings in the cricketing world. Suamy sported a light suit which offset his graying temples. The camera caught a few shiny spots on his forehead as he leaned forward and pointed with his pen to accentuate his words.

'This week we saw a remarkable performance from a young cricketer. Performances like these have been seminal events in the past and we may be seeing the emergence of the future of Indian cricket. I had applauded the selectors on their bold step in including Arjun in the Challenger trophy games before he had even played a single first class game. I now challenge them to take it further and blood him on the forthcoming tour to Pakistan. The maturation process of one so young and so talented can be greatly accelerated by exposure to the highest level of the game. The team is being finalized as we speak and I will have my comments on the composition at the end of this show. The other stark truth made apparent by the recent....'

The interest level in the room plummeted and Pranay moved away from the television. Arjun's mother brought in hot *batata wadas*. Pausing to stuff one into his mouth, Pranay asked, 'So what do you think? Do you have a shot at making the team?'

Arjun looked confused. The emotions of yesterday's game still ran high and he truthfully had not thought beyond it. Certainly a place in the national side had not crossed his brimming mind. 'I don't know! It seems like yesterday when the Bombay schools' side seemed out of reach.'

Pallavi had been chomping at the bit and now would not be denied. 'Actually you would be the eighth right hand batsman in the side. That is if you make the eleven and statistics have shown that sides with four or more left hand batsmen have won more Test matches.'

Arjun glared at her impatiently. 'Why don't you call the selectors? I'm sure they will appreciate your scientific input.' Their attention was grabbed by the television again. The commercials had ceded to Pavaskar who was saying,

'I have before me India's team for the Pakistan tour.' Given to dialogues with the idiot box, Pallavi quipped, 'Then hurry and tell us!'

Arjun leaned forward, 'Sssh!'

Saumil continued, 'The team is well balanced, right and left handed batsmen...'

Pranay couldn't resist prodding Pallavi in the ribs. 'You must be pleased Pallu!'

Arjun externalized his edginess. 'Would you guys shut up!'

'Spinners and pacers.' Pavaskar looked down at the paper in front of him.

'And a wicket keeper or two. Tell us something we don't know,' Pranay added helpfully.

Unable to concentrate and needing an outlet for the tension that was building up within him Arjun threw a cushion at him. Pranay put his finger on his lips promising to be silent. Finally Pavaskar reached the meat of the matter.

'And I am sorry to say that the selectors have been singularly unimaginative. Thirteen players select themselves in my mind. The selectors should have made the 14th and 15th slots count. Bring in some building blocks to work on a foundation for the future. The selectors have ignored upcoming batsmen like Arjun Athavale from Mumbai, pacers like Tamil Nadu's...'

Pallavi jumped up and hugged her brother. 'I am so sorry! Maybe I jinxed you with all that right-hand, left-hand talk.'

Fighting back tears Arjun looked away and mumbled. 'It's all right. A few hours ago I hadn't even thought of it. It was only after Pavaskar mentioned it. It was a long shot anyway. I have had a dizzy ride, and it was only because...' His words trailed off as he struggled to maintain composure.

Pranay quickly intervened, 'Will you stop that! You played well. You will get your opportunity. Give yourself some credit. Besides, you will be a fixture in the Ranji side now. How many kids our age can say that?'

Suamy was not done yet. The mention of his name drew Arjun's attention back to the iridescent image. 'And the only advice I can give young Arjun is perseverance. Talent, he has in oodles. Now he has to learn to live with the ups and downs; not only in his own form but in the vagaries of the selection process.'

Suddenly in no mood to discuss this; Arjun stood up abruptly. 'Time to hit the books. Now I have no excuse for poor grades.'

The EMOTIONAL ROLLER COASTER had a reluctant passenger. The HIGHS could never be fully enjoyed for fear of the ever lurking LOWS.

Yet, the ride was addictive.

And Arjun now saw that LOWS weren't the doldrums, always, sometimes they were a preamble to the exhilarating HIGHS.

He was buckled on for the RIDE.

5

The next few weeks were slow and severe. After the feverish pace of the inter-school and Challenger tournaments, Arjun settled back into a more regular life. He reconnected with his friends and classmates and took to his books with renewed vigour. He even stayed away from the pick-up cricket games in the building compound. Rahim baited him endlessly. Arjun just smiled and walked away. The exams drew closer, the Indian team left for Pakistan. The attendant press coverage replete with articles bemoaning Arjun's exclusion was distracting. Arjun summoned all of his reserves and tried to stay away from newspapers and the television. He buried himself in his books allowing himself only brief moments of 'What if?' daydreams.

The Test series coincided with the examinations. Pallavi was done with her exams and was glued to the telly. She kept Arjun updated with the highlights, statistics and notable happenings of the series. Then, one day, there was a different story in the newspapers. It was the day before his penultimate examination. The final Test match was on. Arjun was relatively well prepared in the next day's subject. He woke up late to be greeted by a solemn silence around the breakfast table. Pallavi had been crying. His father had thin, pursed lips which could only mean seething unreleased anger. His mother hustled around. The bustle and quickly averted eyes betrayed her discomfort. Before he could ask, the headlines on the sports page grabbed his attention. The bold banner read; 'MUMBAI TEEN BOUGHT TICKET TO FAME'.

Arjun grabbed the paper. His eyes darted across the print trying to get the gist of the copy; right in the middle of which was a smiling portrait of him. The words burned his eyes ripping across numerous synapses to bounce against the inside of his skull. In summary, it alleged that a certain Arjun had bought his way into the Challenger trophy squads by bribing the selectors. It ascribed the news to sources that 'preferred to stay anonymous' and though Arjun's performance in that tourney should have got him a spot in the national side; the selectors had left him out for fear that this transaction would come to light. The selectors whom the paper had reached for comments had vehemently denied the allegations. But the Mumbai cricket association had promised an inquiry. Arjun dropped the paper.

'What the fuck!' he shrieked, oblivious to his parents' presence. Pallavi looked up disconcerted. His parents apparently had not heard him. They looked at him tenderly. His mother rushed over and hugged him. His father gazed down at his cooling tea; a teardrop broke the film forming on its surface.

The next week was a nightmare that Arjun sleepwalked through. Pranay and he speculated *ad nauseum* regarding the identity of the anonymous source. The mendacity of the allegations outraged them. The only name they came up with repeatedly was Rahim. Pranay even confronted him. A scornful Rahim maintained that he would seek revenge and retribution on the field and would never resort to something as underhand as this.

That morning they received another phone call from the Mumbai cricket association president confirming that an inquiry would be conducted. Arjun's father asked for Arjun to be excused; as he had his finals. The board chief Manmohan Dalmeinkuchkala relented and allowed his father to appear before an appointed committee. A belligerent Arjun insisted for a while that he would take care of his own problems. Finally he relented, breaking down in his mother's arms.

That night Mr. Athavale stumbled home after finding solace at a familiar place. He gestured his family away and settled in a dark corner. In a few minutes he was retching. Jyoti rushed to his side. She screamed; the vomitus was mainly blood. Arjun came out to assist her. They wiped the inebriated patriarch who was mumbling incoherently and helped him to bed. Mr. Athavale settled into an ungracious slumber. A whispered discussion resulted in a decision to not seek medical attention as long as he slept stably.

Arjun returned to his room disturbed to see his father in such a state. He felt responsible; the recent downturn in family fortunes was largely his doing. His family was paying for his fame. Lying in bed these tumultuous thoughts roller coasted through his frazzled brain. In a fit of rage he rushed over to his kit bag and angrily threw his well-worn gloves out of his window. A few moments later he ran down to retrieve them, clutching them close to his bosom.

Jyoti glanced across at her sleeping husband. His sleep was fitful; familiar demons feasted on his addled brain. She wiped his brow. He should disgust her. But the worst she felt was pity. Mingled with love. She loved this man. A man she had married without thought. Had reconciled herself to a loveless life. She remembered Ulhas, vaguely. The intensity of feeling had faded like a pleasant dream she had vowed to live by. To use as a crutch. She wondered how it would have been if she had made her life with Ulhas. Long ago the hurt from this thought process was searing, visceral. Now it just amused her. She had everything from Anand. A good husband and a devoted father. As regards his shortcomings, she empathized. They both had a past, had lived through the stormy present; he was all she wanted in the future. Anand made a guttural sound. She reached over and made sure he was alright and walked to the bathroom. She stared at her image staring back at her. She mouthed silently, 'He is a kind man. He is good for me.' The dust on the bathroom counter caught her eye. She dabbed her finger in it and penned as only she could.

Jyoti Anand Athavale.

JYOTI SURESH DAMLE

Jyoti Suresh Damle. She could write that name in impeccable cursive whenever called upon. In fact she could remember the day she first wrote it. In 5th grade with a brand new fountain pen her father had bought her from a streetside vendor, who had demonstrated with much fervour that the nib would not break, even if the pen fell directly on it. She had filled her new pen with Royal blue ink carefully using a dropper and was ready for her first class in cursive writing. Sister Antoinette had made them practice letters for a few months but now they were to begin writing words and sentences. For the first class they had to write their name a hundred times. At the end of the period the stern nun walked around and examined the proffered notebooks. A sharp intake of breath as she examined her work alarmed Jyoti Suresh Damle. But the effusive praise that followed caused her to blush till she felt ticklish behind her ears. Sister Antoinette commandeered the book and propped it up inside the notice board for all to see.

'The child is magnificent. Such penmanship is a gift from above,' she gushed.

For a whole week the notebook stayed there. Secretly pleased Jyoti Suresh Damle wrote her name again and again. On the backs of books, on newspapers even on the paper bag her lunch was wrapped in. It became her identity. She didn't feel that Jyoti completely defined her. To be complete she had to be Jyoti Suresh Damle. SHE was Jyoti Suresh Damle. As Jyoti Suresh Damle she won every handwriting competition she entered. Eventually the results of these were so one-sidedly predictable that Lily Fonseca once scribbled 'What's the damn use' across her entry form for which she had to write 'I will try harder next time' two hundred times. One hundred for insubordination and the other hundred for using the word damn. St Mary's convent school for girls had strict rules and an undisputed handwriting champion.

Jyoti Suresh Damle went through school without much fuss. She stayed comfortably behind the top ranked whiz kids. It was not her place to be amongst them. She was a happy girl. Content to belong in the niche provided to her in her class. She was well liked; maybe just short of being popular. Every handwriting contest brought short-lived fame. Jyoti Suresh Damle enjoyed it. She took her matriculation examinations the same year her brother did the intermediate science test. She wrote all her answers in flowing cursive taking great pains to be neat. His results came a week before hers. He had done wonderfully well. His scores ensured him a position in a top medical school. Her father brought home a lot of *pedhas*. The expensive kind covered in granular sugar. She was entrusted with the task of distributing them to neighbours and friends. She made little packets in meticulously cut newspaper pieces, placing the precise number of *pedhas* in each as there were members in the household. As she handed them out everyone asked about her results. 'Not out yet,' she shyly answered. Almost everyone assured her she would do well and demanded that she return with more sweetmeats when that happened. She promised she would. On the day of the results she checked her number in the newspaper. She had passed with a first class. That afternoon she and her classmates were gathered in a hot classroom as Sister Mathilda handed out their marksheets. "Jyoti Shooresh Damli" she called. Trembling a bit the young girl walked up and picked it up. She had scored very well in languages and social sciences but lagged behind the others in mathematics and science.

Her father's disappointment that evening was palpable. He murmured an insincere 'Well done *beta*' as she touched his feet for blessings. That evening he spoke to his wife softly but firmly and proclaimed to his daughter; '*Beta*, I think it is best for you to enroll in Arts. No point in pursuing something if one does not have the natural aptitude for it.' Jyoti Suresh Damle nodded demurely. She had really not thought very far ahead and her father was surely right! As an afterthought her father handed her pedhas that evening to distribute to the neighbors again. They were not the expensive kind. In fact, they felt hard and tasted slightly rancid. "I am going into Arts she told her neighbors. Most of them non-judgmentally blessed her. She heard one older nosy woman murmuring, 'Why Arts? I thought she was a bright girl,' before she was effectively shushed.

The next morning armed with all the requisite paperwork she secured a place in the FY Arts class at the Suryanarayan Maheshwari College in Matunga or the SM College as its students called it. Her major was history and minors, economics and English literature. She was happy that Lily Fonseca was going to be in her English lit. class. Initially, Lily and she traveled to college together walking with bowed heads past the vagrant 'chronics' gathered outside college gates.

'Don't mess with them. They are *asli goondas*,' Lily instructed.

Soon, Lily gravitated to the cooler class-cutting, party-going crowd. Initially, she dragged her friend along, however it was soon apparent that Jyoti Suresh Damle was a misfit in the popular gang and she slowly settled back into her classes now running the gauntlet of the 'chronics' on her own. None of her subjects interested her, but she read enough to do reasonably well in her tests. Lily joined the film society and the student union. She busied herself with student causes and wore a rakish defiant bandana across her forehead.

One morning she accosted her old friend, 'Listen *yaar*. You must do me this favour. We need a writer for a blind student. I don't remember his name. He is taking his final BA exams after our tests are done. You have such beautiful handwriting. You must do this.'

Jyoti Suresh Damle began to protest, but could not come up with a single plausible excuse. 'Settled then' Lily said matter-of-factly. 'Come to the student union office and I will give you the details.'

That evening she stopped by to see Lily who thrust a paper at her.

'Thanks yaar,' she screamed before her attention span gave way. Jyoti Suresh Damle looked at the paper. 'Ulhas Ranade' was scripted unevenly, below which, there was a telephone number.

That evening she called hesitantly.

'Ulhas Ranade please, I am calling in reference to the writer needed for the examination.'

A brief moment later a smiley voice came on, 'This is Ulhas here. I am so glad you called. Lily told me about you. It is great that you have been studying English lit. My writer for the last exam was a science student who substituted saucer for Chaucer. I am sure that paper made no sense.' He paused and laughed at the memory. She smiled at the other end. 'I didn't quite get your name from Lily.'

'Jyoti Suresh Damle,' came the pat reply.

'Now that's a mouthful' he continued. 'Let's meet tomorrow in the canteen. Eleven o'clock all right. You don't have a lecture then, do you? You should recognize me easily. I'll be the blind guy.'

'Eleven is fine,' she replied, 'Okay then,' she continued by way of goodbye and disconnected. She was thoroughly disarmed by his enthusiasm and light hearted chatter. The next morning she sat before a steaming cup of coffee in the canteen when he strode in. A few taps with his cane and he was in the middle of the canteen.

'Jyoti Suresh Damle, are you here.'

A few faces turned as she walked over and tapped his hand.

'I'm here.' Hesitating a bit, she then grasped his elbow and led him to her table. He settled down and ordered a coffee.

'We have a month between your test and my finals. Will you be able to spend some time with me between now and then? I would like you to get used to my diction and we can make any adjustments, if required.'

'Sure,' she assented. 'Why, even before if you...'

'Okay then, Friday evening in the film society office. It's a date. Don't forget, now at least you will be able to recognize me.'

Up till then, Jyoti Suresh Damle had looked down at her coffee. She abruptly looked up. She needed to look into his eyes. Hazel and brown, his eyes were downcast. They tittered nervously in their sockets till they twinkled. She didn't believe it at first, but they twinkled again.

'Are you looking at my eyes?' he asked. They twinkled again.

'Yes,' she replied.

'Good,' he went on, twinkle twinkle. 'Now I feel like we have connected.' Abruptly, he pushed his chair back and got up waving her helping hand away. 'Till Friday then,' and strode away. She finished her coffee in silence, nonplussed.

In the next few days it seemed like he was everywhere. She would catch sight of him striding, always striding; a few inquisitive taps with his cane and he plunged ahead. Not the shuffling gait of the insecure unsighted for him. She found herself stopping and staring, then gathering herself only to stare again, her curiousity secure in his blindness. When he faltered, she gasped but stayed away; watching this magnificient, confident man. She met him as planned on Friday. Without any preamble he launched forth.

'You must be wondering what I have to do with the film society. I mean being blind and all. I love movies. I can sit and listen to them, sense them and they are always flawless. Of course not the crass Hindi ones. Because, I imagine them like I want to; so the filmmaker's follies are wiped away. In fact, I get more pleasure out of them, than most others.'

Jyoti Suresh Damle was content to listen. She was in awe of his knowledge, his verve; just everything about him. He always called her by her full name; he sensed that this was her individuality, her distinctness. They met more often. He spoke, she wrote. He loved the beauty of words and wrapped his narrative with them. She grew to love literature; she saw it through his eyes. He gave her books to read and quizzed her about them. Byron, Tagore, Shelley and Shakespeare. He spent a lot of time in the British council library with its extensive Braille collection and recorded works. Jyoti Suresh Damle grew her third dimension.

His exams came and went. He was anxious about her handwriting. That was the one time she could confidently reassure him. He would graduate that year and had an assistant's job at the British council library in hand. They knew him, loved him and were happy to have him. Ulhas and Jyoti spent as much time together as they could.

The film society had its annual festival. They sweated through 'Pather Panchali', 'Bicycle Thieves' and 'Z'. They traveled to south Bombay together. He insisted on traveling in the gents' compartment and would not hear of her coming along. She fearfully watched him get on and rushed to him at Churchgate. They spent time together at his house. She would help his mother fix lunch and the three of them would listen to old Frank Sinatra and Connie Francis songs on the gramophone. Of course the neighbors talked. Someone saw them coming out of a cinema house. Another reported them to be snuggling over a *lassi* at Kailash Parbat. Her mother questioned her. Jyoti Suresh Damle always confidently replied that she knew what she was doing and demanded some trust; some understanding from her family. Luckily her authoritarian father was blissfully unaware.

Ulhas started his job; she started her second year at college. They went on hikes together; she boldly led him; while he lifted his nose in the air to smell the first rain, the jasmine blossoms. They went to the movies together. His uncanny sense of prop placement, lighting in the scenes always left her wonderstruck. He saw so much more than she did.

'*Retinitis pigmentosa*, that's what I have,' he said, one day out of the blue. 'I was twelve when it started, fourteen when I couldn't see anymore.'

She was startled; she had always thought that Ulhas had been blind from birth. To have once seen and now to know what one couldn't? It was enough to drive her into a deep depression. How then, why then; was he so upbeat? Sensing her thoughts he spoke, 'Remorse…, remorse and regret are the two most useless emotions. It's not easy but I choose to be optimistic, positive, and cheery.' He turned away; it may have been a tear or an errant speck of dust. He wiped his eyes.

They went to the movies and watched Roman Holiday. She impulsively reached for his hand and guided it around her. He let it lay there limp till she pulled it down to her breast. There was a sharp sound, anguish and ecstasy as she placed his sensitive fingertips on her attentive nipple. They sat motionless as he tentatively probed uncharted territory. Then she pulled his face to him and kissed him like she had seen Sophia Loren do in the movies. He pulled away not quite pleased with the turn of events; not displeased either. Disquieted, yet helpless against the riptide of burgeoning emotion. The 'chronics' heckled them. *'Dekh, dekh, Surdas aur uska maal.'*. *'Saala main bhi andha hota yaar, koi toh mujhse bhi aise hi chipak jaati.'*. They hissed deprecatingly. 'Ignore them,' he pleaded. She walked on, head high, cheeks burning. Not from shame but from a seething wrath that would have ground the silly smiling faces to pulp. They shortened her name to 'Surdas Ka Maal' or 'SKM'. Cruel hisses of SSSSkm assaulted her. Lily came to her one day.

'What is this man? I almost think it's my fault. You know, like, I got you into the paper-shaper writing thing.'

Jyoti Suresh Damle assured her that all was well. That she knew what she was doing; pushing her well-meaning friend away. Ulhas wrote her letters. Short letters. Loving, caring letters in a sloping hand that slanted across the page. She kept them, read them and reread them along with Steinbeck, Tennessee Williams and Gabriel Garcia Marquez. She bloomed, oh how she bloomed.

One evening she returned from college; the second year was almost over. Her father sat sternly at the dining table; her mother was nowhere to be seen. Choked crying from the inside bedroom gave her whereabouts away.

'It's got to stop. I don't want to hear anything. S.T.O.P. Am I clear?' he threw down a piece of paper on the table and stalked away to quieten his spouse. Jyoti Suresh Damle picked it up and opened up the crumpled chit. The familiar sloping hand gazed back at her.

'Dearest Jyoti Suresh Damle. First stop crying. You know it had to end. Your father is right; nothing against me but where is the compatibility? Thank you for being a friend and always, smile! It makes you look pretty and the world around you happy.'

She bunched the note up and charged out of the house. She didn't stop till she reached his door. A red-eyed Mrs. Ranade answered the door.

'Please leave him alone,' she pleaded. 'Your father has said enough. Go away and think about it for a while. Ulhas has to deal with his fate, his destiny; I can only cushion it. It is hard enough without this constant corrosion of self esteem. Please go away now.' As the distraught girl walked away she felt unseeing eyes watching her. She tried to contact him repeatedly; finally he agreed to meet her. They met for coffee. His wary mother dropped him and waited in the lobby of the five-star hotel as they took their seats in the coffee shop. He looked a bit gaunt but otherwise outwardly jolly.

'You know he is right. Your father is right. What can I offer you, except for one more person to care for?' She just teared up.

'Does what I want, matter? Do I have any say?' Her thoughts went back to the day she had bought him her first gift. Rip-off Ray-ban shades from one of the Malayalee vendors near VT. She was surprised at his rage.

'So you want me to hide them. To cover them up. My eyes are unseeing. Does that make them unsightly? The world is uncomfortable looking into my eyes so I should cover them? Do you hide all your wounds? Little scars from scrapes, big wounds on your soul those are just as plain to see? Bah!'

'No, I didn't mean it that way. I just thought...' she had whimpered.

'Thought what, that dark glasses are an optimal gift for a blind man. I won't wear my affliction like a badge,' he had roared. His mortification was complete and compelling.

She had burst into tears and charged home. He had apologized profusely and refused to return the glasses. He would flash them on briefly on occasion, if only for her to protest and half heartedly try to grab them. He wanted to show her that he valued her. Valued her enough to wear the reprehensible gift. She was jarred back to the present, as he took her hand.

'It is for the best. I can't fight the world and don't choose to have you do so. Can we move on? Maybe we can put all this behind us and be friends. Good friends, someday. I would like that. We could even go to the movies together. I promise no *masti*.' He smiled and she wept deep wracking eye-turning sobs. He got up. The rendezvous was done. He wiped away a tear and looked Jyoti Suresh Damle square in the eye and said, 'Smile, smile won't you. That's how I want to remember you.' She could not hold back her heaving grief. It was like a heavy stone crushing everything that she had to live for. The hovering waiter tactfully disappeared. She walked over to watch him stride down the stairs. He raised his hand and waved and beckoned her. She ran down.

'RP, *retinitis pigmentosa*, it is hereditary. I can't wish this fate on anyone else,' he announced.

With renewed vigor she blurted out, 'We won't have kids. I'll get my tubes tied. Is that all you think I want?'

He looked back, 'No, it's what I think you deserve.' He reached into his pocket and pulled out the shades. Beat up Ray-bans with scratched dark green glasses; placed them on his nose and walked over to his waiting mother with an exaggerated shuffle.

Jyoti caught up with him silently. She held him back with a firm grip on his elbow. 'It can't end like this. I am not ready. I want to spend some time with you.' 'SOME TIME!' How innocuous that sounded. Her meaning was clear to both of them. He didn't say no, but walked away. Jyoti called his mother. Her mind was full of potential excuses. They weren't needed. She showed up at the predetermined hour. Ulhas let her in and walked back to his room. She followed him, pausing to look around the house. To drink it all in. She had pictured the rest of her life in this house.

He was sitting on the edge of the bed. She hesitated as the dappled sunlight bounced off his face. She slipped out of her clothes before walking over to him. She picked up his hand and caressed her body with it. Ulhas let out a stifled groan. He was crying. She wiped his eyes lovingly. There was no twinkle. Only misery. She lay down next to him as he fumbled with his clothes. She waited patiently, intuitively knowing that he would be hurt if she helped him. He turned to her and she felt him rub against her thigh. Suddenly with a sharp intake of breath he moaned softly. 'Sorry.' he said. She felt the spreading warmth on her thigh. She lay there in his arms for a while. He looked away; his unseeing eyes were fixated on the far wall. She kissed his eyes as she rolled onto him, guiding his hands to her breasts. This time there was nothing hurried. Now he would always be a part of her.

As she left the room, she looked back and smiled. She wanted him to remember her that way.

Jyoti Suresh Damle met suitor after suitor listlessly. Her parents paraded them before her with frantic urgency. She met the USA-returned ones and the landowners from Satara. Her lifeless apathy turned one and all away. Savitri *kaki* was called for an urgent consultation. 'Marriage will only bring her added responsibilities,' she proclaimed. 'She will be happiest single. But if she marries her children will be her sole joy.'

One evening another prospective groom and his family came over. He had a wobbly gait and glazed eyes. Jyoti Suresh Damle's mother made masala tea and *pohe* garnished with fresh coriander and grated coconut. The main protagonists were lackadaisical about the meeting. She saw a kind smile; he saw double. A few days later the prospective groom's family communicated approval of the match. The bride-to-be's opinion beyond a 'He will do, right' was not solicited. The wedding date was finalized. She begged for one last meeting with Ulhas. She wanted to tell him about the wedding herself. Maybe…Face to face….Maybe Ulhas would relent. He might just… Her father refused. The next day he returned and handed her a note.

'I went over and dropped off an invitation' he explained.

She opened up the note to the familiar sloping slanting hand.

'Dear Jyoti Suresh Damle, I wish you happiness and only happiness always. Have no regrets. I don't. Just smile… I'll be thinking of you.'

She folded it away carefully. On her wedding day she pulled out both notes and studied them. She turned them over and pulled out her favorite pen. Jyoti Anand Athavale she wrote in her best cursive. Jyoti Anand Athavale she wrote again and again till the words jumbled up and the paper was covered by a hodge-podge of letters. She looked down and thought.

'I can write that well. I can write Jyoti Anand Athavale well.' She tore up the notes and went to the *mandap* dry eyed.

Arjun spent a sleepless night and woke up bleary eyed. Pallavi gently reminded him about his exams. Chagrin was quickly replaced by panic. Arjun attempted a last minute cram. The test that day was therapeutic. It forced him to think and did not allow him to dwell on the unfair rap.

Two days later, his father gathered up all his bank records and financial transactions and trudged off to face the inquisitors. They pored over his records, questioned transactions, mulled on the answers and finally released his father late in the evening. An unspoken pact prevailed at home. No one discussed the allegations or the probe. It was like an elephant in their living room that everyone walked around. Arjun finished his last exam and did surprisingly well. The Indian team tasted bitter defeat in the final test. The series had been closely fought; finally the home team prevailed 2-1. The deciding test had two drastic batting collapses by the Indian side; again igniting the debate surrounding Arjun's exclusion. His proponents pleaded prodigal talent; their opponents held out Arjun's inexperience. Arjun, meanwhile stuck to his books.

A few days later, the headlines screamed again. 'MUMBAI TEEN EXONERATED OF BRIBERY CHARGES.' No evidence had been found against Arjun, no action was to be taken. That afternoon, a contrite Dalmeinkuchkala visited Arjun and his family and personally apologized for the inconvenience. Just after he left, Arjun buried his face in his gloves and cried bitter tears. He should have felt relieved but all he could summon was a hollow void.

Two days later the newspaper published a retraction. Ostensibly their anonymous source was not as reliable as initially deemed. Friends and well-wishers urged Arjun's father to sue, but the poor middle class tippler had had enough; choosing to forgive and forget.

The RIDE continued. Unlike amusement fair rides, there was no getting off this real LIFE ride. One had to enjoy it or grin and bear it. There was no other mantra for survival.

Arjun was perplexed by the lack of GRAYS in his world. He was now a master of the steep dips into the LOWS. The WHITES and the BLACKS, the YES and the NOS. Many absolutes. Not too many MAYBES or GRAYS.

He craved them. With GRAYS there was HOPE. MAYBES were possibilities. Not being ABSOLUTE they needed no REASON. And he didn't have to question them. Tease them to unravel.

6

 The Test series did inspire some interest. But most fans just followed the scores. Few could afford the time to watch the five-day long drawn out affairs. However, they did serve as a prelude to the one-day series. This brand of instant cricket attracted many more viewers. The first of the one-day matches was to begin at Sialkot and although all things cricket had been taboo in the Athavale household for a while, Pallavi duly tuned in a few minutes before the game was to begin.

Rabi Mantri was commenting, holding a wireless microphone looking directly into the camera.

'Good morning ladies and gentlemen! Welcome to Sialkot. We have a great day of cricket lined up for you. The weather gods have been kind. The temperate weather and easy wicket should allow the batsmen to make their shots while a bit of moisture in the track following yesterday's showers should aid the seamers early. Joining me now is ex-India great Sujay Wandrekar. The camera panned over to his partner in the commentary box. Sujay Wandrekar blushed before self effacingly continuing, 'Just ex-India! But the conditions here today favor a scintillating display from current and future India greatest! None other than Suchen Chemburkar.' 'Tell me Sujay! What would you do if you had won the toss?' Mantri queried.

'Great question! Difficult to answer. It is tempting to put the other side in; given that the only assistance to the bowlers may be early on...' Wandrekar began.

'That's a moot point. Gourav called it right and has asked Pakistan to bat. One can't help thinking back to the last time he did this in the World Cup finals. That one ended disastrously for India. Here's Sainath with the first ball...' Mantri took over.

The Pakistani batsmen dominated the morning's play. None of the Indian bowlers could make any impression and the men in green scored at will. Their skipper Azam stood tall and led the way. Mercifully for the Indian bowlers, the allotted 50 overs eventually ended. Pakistan finished with 282 for 6.

The commentary team grudgingly praised the Pakistani effort. Mantri signed off with, 'What a glorious innings from Azam! 282 may just be out of India's reach. However, they do have the stroke players! See you at 1 pm local time when play resumes with India batting.'

The Indian innings started disastrously losing two wickets in the first over. Suchen and Nakul David steadied the boat. Nakul, the anchor of the middle order batted steadily, grafting runs with pushes and prods; indulging in the sporadic hit to the fence off bad deliveries. Suchen was lucky to survive; looking distinctly uncomfortable facing up to balls on and around the off, swinging away. Riding lady luck he soon warmed to the task at hand. The score slowly inched to 230 for 2 after 42 overs. Azam turned to his quickest bowler in a last ditch attempt to save the game.

The first ball reared up from a good length and made contact with the back of Suchen's hand as he tried to fend it away. The crunching sound was sickening and Suchen slowly crumpled down. The fielder at gully charged up and gobbled the ballooning ball. For the millions of India fans the scene unfolded in slow motion. Nakul gestured to the umpire and rushed down the wicket to the aid of his fallen comrade. The crowd fell silent as the players gathered around Suchen. Back in the commentary box the Indians worked on their fingernails, attempting to keep their comments professional and non-partisan.

'That was a nasty blow! That is the hand he had surgery on earlier this year. He is wringing his hand trying to work off the pain. He is gesturing to the pavilion. He has just realized that he is not just injured, but also out, caught at gully. What a blow for India. Just when they seemed to be cruising to victory. Will this turn the tide?' Mantri reported.

The game recommenced, but the blow suffered by the bastion of the batting lineup, had deflated the team's spirit. Nakul held his end up and tried to keep the scoreboard moving. However there was a parade back to the pavilion at the other end. The valiant effort finally came to an end and the innings folded at 278 for 8 in 50 overs.

In his concluding remarks that evening Mantri reported; 'What a finish! One can't help feeling that the result would have been different if a certain Mr. Chemburkar had been around till the end. Here is an update on his injury. X-rays show no fracture. But he is in tremendous pain. He has a tear in the webbing between his fingers that has required stitches. The team management and he have decided that he will return to India to sort it out. It is rumored that Gourav has specifically asked for young Mumbai batsman Arjun Athavale to be sent as a replacement.'

Wandrekar had this to add. 'That is decidedly unusual; to specifically request a particular player. Usually the decision is left to the selectors. I just hope that Arjun has been practicing. Luckily for him those baseless bribery charges are a thing of the past. Perhaps Gourav was influenced by that spectacular innings in the Challenger trophy finals. He had the opportunity of witnessing it first hand from the other end. We will now say goodbye and will be with you again on Tuesday from Lahore for the second ODI...'

Pallavi let out a signature scream and rushed around the room screaming

'Arjun is going to Pakistan,' at the top of her voice. The din brought her mother out of the kitchen.

'What's going on?' Before Pallavi could elaborate the telephone rang urgently. Looking bewildered Arjun's mother wiped her brow with her sari, picked up the telephone and diffidently spoke, 'Hello! Yes I remember, you had called before...Singh. That's right... Ram Singh from CBA.... I'm sorry BCA. YES, he is not in right now. I'll have him call you. Wait a minute here he comes.'

Arjun entered the room and quizzically surveyed the scene before him. He took the proffered phone, 'Yes! Good evening sir! No, I haven't heard anything. Are you sure? Of course it won't be a problem. I will check with my parents. How soon? I am ready now! Oh! Formalities. Visa and all. OK I'll be there.'

Now completely confused his mother pleaded for an explanation.

'What was that all about?'

Not one to beat around the bush, a beaming Arjun came right out, 'Aai! I'm going to Pakistan!'

'But officially we haven't..', Pallavi urged caution.

Arjun shushed her with a slight gesture and continued. 'It is official. There is going to be a press conference this evening. I am to get an emergent visa, and will probably fly out in two days. Won't make it in time for the second ODI; doesn't matter. I probably won't play unless there are more injuries.'

This was all too sudden for his mother. She sat down heavily on the sofa holding her head. 'But Pakistan! Alone!'

Arjun walked over to his mother and hugged her. 'Now don't start that *Aai*! I will be fine.' His reassurance couldn't keep the tears from springing to her eyes. She wanted to share in her son's happiness; but he was so young!

The next few days were busy, 'good busy'. Arjun flew around with the wind in his feet. Happy days were here again. He smiled his way through the visa formalities and the well-meaning pointers that most senior cricketers were intent on sharing with him. Arjun packed his soiled gloves carefully along with a spanking new kit; a thoughtful gift from friends and relatives. Of course, the hidden agenda was a share of some of the reflected glory for any great feats on Arjun's part in the future.

Arjun could not watch the second game. He had to attend a press conference. He deferred most of the questions posed to him to Mr. Dalmeinkuchkala and seemed content to smile nonchalantly into the cameras. He returned that afternoon to catch the end of the game.

An unusually morose Rabi Mantri somberly spoke. 'Another gut wrenching loss for the Indians. The Indians demonstrated tremendous grit going into the game without their key batsman, Suchen Chemburkar; but came up just short again. They need to turn things around and quickly or it will all be over; whether or not the fat lady has sung. Someone needs to provide the spark.'

That evening Arjun rechecked his bag a few times, ensuring that the gloves were still there. Pallavi hovered, while her mother returned repeatedly with new parcels that she secreted into his bags. Finally, the family set out for the airport in a cab. Pranay had to bid goodbye earlier than anticipated as the cabbie refused to tempt fate or an unwelcome *havaldar* by taking a fifth passenger, even though he was ferrying the newest star on the Indian cricket firmament. Rahim showed up and reluctantly waved, as the cab emerged from the building gate. He was proud of his compatriot but just a wee bit jealous too. Pakya and his cronies had lined up to salute their hero. This overwhelming show of solidarity brought tears to Arjun's eyes. He wiped them hastily as Pallavi looked at him closely to see if he was lacrimating.

The cab dropped them in the midst of a moderate crowd outside the airport. A loud group was wailing inconsolably as a smartly dressed young man patiently alternated between being garlanded and touching feet. A harried *havaldar* attempted to bring some order to the chaos by moving the reluctant cars along. A few folks turned around half-recognizing Arjun from his grainy newspaper pictures. Manmohan Dalmeinkuchkala and Ram Singh Kullarpur were already at the airport and rushed over to greet him. New to situations like these, Arjun awkwardly bid *adieu* and turned to his outwardly stoic family. Arjun bent down and sought blessings from his parents, looking up to reassure his mother.

'Yes *Aai*, I will be careful. There are people to guide me and tell what to do.'

His mother stuck to her agenda and rattled off last minute instructions, 'If you don't like the food, don't forget the *chaklis* and *ladoos* I have packed. Remember, if you are in a bind, Rashid *chacha* is in Pakistan for his leather business. I have given you his contact details. You kept them safely *na*?'

'If I get them through customs; they may have restrictions you know,' warned Arjun, his mind on the ladoos. He patted his pocket to assure his mother that he had the information.

Pallavi clamored for attention. 'And don't try to pull the left arm spinners; your high back lift is all wrong for that.'

A wave of awkwardness swept through him. He needed to get going. He hugged his family once again and stepped away. 'I really must go now.'

Pallavi wasn't done yet. 'Lead with your left elbow and drop the bottom hand if the ball moves away.' Arjun walked away. He looked back and saw his father break away from his family and walk towards him, like he had unfinished business.

'Listen *bachcha*,' he walked up to his son and handed him a packet. He pulled his son towards him and whispered urgently. 'Believe in yourself. It's all in you. All those performances; they came from within you. You are solely in control. If you come to realize this, use those.' With this he gestured to the packet Arjun clutched in his hands. Overcome, Arjun abruptly walked away and disappeared into the terminal without another look behind.

The formalities were endless, but the staff at the counters recognized him and expedited his progress to the airplane. Arjun finally settled into his seat and being a first time flier attempted to familiarize himself with the plethora of buttons, knobs, lights, compartments and instructions that assailed him from all directions.

He adjusted his hand luggage holding his father's packet in his hand for a bit; looking at it curiously. Finally he opened the bag gingerly and peered into it. A new pair of batting gloves looked back at him. Arjun looked at them, smiled and packed them into his hand luggage. For all his absent-mindedness [not knowing that his glasses were perched on the top of his head, while looking for them] his father was pretty astute. He settled down and adjusted his seatbelt and waited to see if the seat next to him was going to be occupied. The plane took off; the seat next to him stayed empty. He spread out a little bit and curled up fighting to stay awake for the meal and in-flight entertainment. When the steward finally came by Arjun was fast asleep, dreaming of photo finishes. His dazzling stroke-play marched his side resolutely to victory. The last ball was coming up. He took his stance as a tall, dark, strapping bowler wearing a turban and a *pathan* suit trundled in. Arjun looked down at his hands. They were bare, his gloves had disappeared. He turned to see a slithery snake disappear into a hole in the ground with them. He looked up. The bowler was in his bowling stride; the ball left his hand. He let the ball loose. It hissed like a snake and bounced on the ground. It did not rear up as expected. It had disappeared! Into the ground. Arjun let out a gasp and woke up drenched in a cold sweat. A quick look around him confirmed that it had been a dream. Pakistan, all by himself! Apprehension gnawed his inside. Well at least Rashid *chacha* was around if he had any serious problem. He pulled his blanket around him and waited for the flight to reach Karachi.

Vikram Dravid

Rashid

Rashid still remembered the tattered old *lungi*. It's green and blue plaid pattern and peculiar wrinkles. He saw it in his mind now as clearly as he saw it that day. His father had asked him to take the day off from classes to accompany him to the hospital. A hacking cough had plagued him for a while but when the sudden weight loss set in he found it impossible to work. Though not quite bed-ridden, he had been an invalid for a few months, waiting for appointments for all his tests. A chest X-ray showed a spot on his lungs and he had been taking some anti-tuberculosis medications. He insisted he felt better but the spot did not go away. He was going to get it biopsied that day. The doctor had told him that they would be able to tell right away. He had also cautioned him to bring somebody along with him. The procedure could incapacitate him temporarily.

Rashid was impatient. He could not understand why his father could not take a taxi to and fro from the hospital. Besides, the test was scheduled just when he had planned to meet his buddies in the college canteen. One silver lining was that he could miss classes. His father insisted on wearing a *lungi*. He said that he didn't have the energy to change. Rashid offered to help. The *lungi* did typify them ethnically, particularly now that his father had decided to grow his beard. Not that he was ashamed; it just seemed wise not to flaunt it.

They had to wait till his father finished his morning prayers to set off. They were late and Rashid wished they would take a cab. His father patiently waited in the sun, squinting up at the bus numbers. At least at the ones that stopped at their stop. Some just whizzed by carrying weary passengers who had won the first battle of the day. Living in the city was a war and there were many skirmishes everyday. Getting onto a bus was certainly a minor victory. Finally a half empty bus stopped and they clambered on. The bus lurched away from the pavement and his father missed a step; leaning back on him for support. Rashid guided him to an empty seat and stood beside him. Their ride was short and the bus deposited them outside the hospital. Rashid's father let out a sigh. He knew the hospital all too well. With a confidence borne from familiarity he navigated the bustling hallways. His gawky son followed a few steps behind him.

A dusty neon sign had the word 'Radiology' painted in bold capital red letters on it. Curiously the paint on both the 'O's in the radiology had peeled off. A harried matron wearing a starched cap asked them to sit and fill up a form. The room smelt of antiseptic and vomit. The blend was somehow comforting. Rashid handed the form in. This room was pleasantly sparse and they were the only occupants. A *jamun* tree heavy with fruit kissed the dusty window which had been propped open slightly. Bustling noisy medical students passed by frequently. It must be time for morning classes. Rashid remembered the definite revulsion he felt. He had no desire to be there or to ever be a part of this process. Death and disease or the threat of it seemed to linger around every corner.

His father was summoned. A bright young man with kind eyes took him away from Rashid.

'You can wait. It will be about thirty minutes. Or you can go have some tea or whatever.'

'Kind eyes' disappeared with his shuffling father and the door shut. Rashid waited. He did not want to explore the outside and though his throat was parched he was sure he would get lost if he strayed far. A busy sweaty man wheeled in a microscope about fifteen minutes later and disappeared through the same door. Kind eyes returned.

'We are all done. Your father is just getting a chest X-ray to make sure that there is no air leak. I want you to wait here with him. The pathologist will take a quick look and tell us if he needs anything more.'

'It's TB right?' Rashid heard his own voice. It then spoke to him, silently. What else could it be? And now with the new drugs it could be completely cured! Rashid remembered Mustafa's grandmother. She had wasted to a stick and had made a full turnaround. Why, just last week he had some fabulous *gosht* she had cooked.

His father returned. He seemed fine outwardly. They exchanged a smile as they settled down. Rashid looked at him out of the corner of his eyes. It must be TB. There was a thin film of sweat on his father's forehead. He resisted the temptation to wipe it. His father looked resolutely ahead. 'Kind eyes' returned and introduced himself.

'Hello, I am Anand. I am a medical student. Senior medical student. The biopsy was successful but we now need a CAT scan.' His father's shoulders drooped. Another test. Rashid extended a hand.

'Rashid Poonawala.' Anand had a firm grip. 'I am reading commerce at Lajpatrai.' Rashid added the latter lamely. Anand nodded, smiled and continued. 'We have an opening right now and I would like to go ahead and get it done.' Rashid's father nodded a hasty acquiescence and pulled himself up. 'You can wait here. This will be quicker.' Anand said to Rashid over his shoulder as he walked out with his father.

Rashid was restless and paced around the room. The cheery voices and bustle outside the window had died down. A dark cloud had shrouded the sun and the air was heavy with potential rain. Rashid felt uncomfortably hot and stood below the slow dusty fan. He undid a few buttons and blew down his shirt front. His day was done. It was not worth the commute to get to college only for the last class. He wished he knew what his friends were doing after classes so he could plan on joining them.

Anand returned with his father. His father clasped Anand's hand familiarly. 'Beta. Will someone tell me what these tests showed? I want to get treatment and get better.' Anand seemed hesitant.

'Well, usually we let your doctor know and then...' He looked into those old beseeching eyes. 'I'll talk to the big doctor. Maybe he can spare a few minutes.' Anand returned immediately and beckoned them to follow him. Dr. Desai was portly. So portly, that the desk before him was pushed away. He looked up and gestured to them to sit.

'*Abba*. You have cancer. The biopsy showed it. And the Cat scan showed that it has spread. Do you smoke a lot?' Rashid's father held his ears and stuck his tongue out nodding his head to vehemently deny the question.

'Never touched a cigarette or a *bidi*. Cancer...' Rashid came to. Thinking back he could never remember what he was thinking about then.

'Can we treat it?' He sputtered.

'Sure, chemotherapy, radiation; but for that you have to go to Tata hospital.' Dr. Desai stopped and took in their attire.

'Very expensive also. Even with that six months maximum.'

Rashid looked at his father. His face was indecipherable. The lines criss-crossing his brow were knotted in a pattern of sorrow and foreboding. At that moment he hated the fat doctor more than anybody. Rashid jumped up.

'We will do it. We will get all the treatment. Abu, leave it to me.'

Dr. Desai was already looking away from them. Rashid led his father out and looked back. 'Kind eyes' eyes were filled with tears. The urge to sob seized him. He swallowed it. They were walking out of the building into the sun which had made a triumphant return.

'*Beta*. Let's get some tea. I want a hot cup of tea with *khari* to dip in it.'

His father strode forward through the milling crowd purposefully. They passed a tea shop. Rashid pointed to it but his father gestured ahead. They were in line for an elevator. The line snaked around a corner and they patiently awaited their turn. Rashid wanted to say something comforting, but what? Everything he could think of, sounded hollow. At that moment he wanted to hold the frail old man and reassure him. Why didn't he?

The lime green elevator doors opened and an attendant dressed in dirty white shorts and shirt with a Nehru cap covering his head let them in. The doors closed noisily. The attendant pressed the requested buttons and settled down on his stool. Rashid looked down and saw bulging veins in his calf. These he always remembered. The bulging veins pulsing like a coiled serpent while the elevator ascended.

They got off on the 5th floor and entered a cafeteria obviously intended for medical students, nurses and doctors. Unperturbed, Rashid's father led him to a corner table and settled down. Immediately, a snotty kid attended on them. He wiped the table while taking their order. Rashid's father sipped his tea noisily; dipping the flaky biscuits in them till his fingertips were also submerged.

'How is your college going *beta*?'

The question was so innocuously out of place in the current context, that Rashid could only muster an 'Ok.'

'*Beta*, you must be more serious now. You are going have to take charge soon.' His father's voice never quavered. Rashid remembered this too. 'Really soon.'

And his father laughed as he said that. Laughed! Rashid looked at his tea unable to respond. His father pushed his chair back.

'*Beta*, I have to go to the bathroom. It's on the next floor. I'll be right back.' He shuffled away.

Rashid sipped his tea thoughtfully. He looked up. 'Kind eyes' was at the next table with a pretty girl. He caught Rashid's glance and smiled. He pointed to his friend and said 'Soma'.

'Rashid' introduced himself and answered 'Gone to the bathroom,' to the inquiringly raised brows. Rashid set down his empty cup. He saw something out of the corner of his eye. He turned, but there was nothing there. Suddenly there was a lot of shouting. It came from below them. Everyone rushed to the window. Rashid found Anand and Soma squeezed in next to him. A crowd of people had gathered gesticulating noisily. A trickle of dark fluid trailed away from them. That's when Rashid saw it.

He saw it and screamed. Screamed then wailed. He pushed the others and rushed madly. He took the broad flight of stairs; charging down. People looked at his agitated face and stepped aside. Rashid pushed the milling people aside. The blue and green plaid lungi was askew. Scrawny buttocks stared up at him. The limbs were in an anatomically impossible arrangement. The face was turned away from him. He sunk to his knees. His trembling hands pulled down the lungi. Modesty was restored. The crowd surged around, drawn to the macabre and grisly. A voice said, 'It will be a police case. Don't touch anything.'

He wanted to scream. 'It's my fucking father.' But he looked up silently. The crowd parted again. Anand and Soma rushed in. The voice repeated his warning. Anand disregarded it. He cradled the head and put it in his lap. His hands were careful, caring, tender. He felt for a pulse. His downcast eyes said it all. He looked up at Rashid and wept. That is when Rashid realized what he had seen out of the corner of his eye. It was an upturned face hurtling down. The eyes were unafraid. Weary, but unafraid.

Later, Rashid often wondered when his father decided to take his own life. Was it when the corpulent Dr. Desai was spelling out the cost and the dismal prognosis? Was it before or after he decided to have tea? Did he talk to him about his responsibilities before or after he had decided? Did he choose the 5th floor cafeteria with this in mind? Or was it just when he had finished using the bathroom? Was it a momentous decision? Was it that he just could not resist the invitation of the wide open window?

Rashid never asked himself why. Just when?

It was a few months later that Rashid met Anand again. There was a commotion at the bus stop as Rashid walked by. He peered through the crowd and saw a young man holding his hand to a bloody cheek. He was about to turn away when he saw the kind eyes. Kind, fearful yet enraged eyes. He pushed his way through.

'Doctor, what happened? What is the matter?' Anand did not recognize him right away. He squinted and the dawn of recognition flitted across his eyes.

'Some guy picked my pocket. I was getting onto the bus when I felt someone reach into my back pocket. I confronted him and he slashed me across my face.'

He dropped his hand and bared a long superficial cut that was still trickling blood. The blood trickled to his chin where it formed a drop. The drop quivered but stayed on the chin. Rashid handed him his handkerchief. Anand pressed it on to the gash.

'I did not see him clearly. But I am sure he is one of those guys.' Anand pointed to a bunch of rough young men who gazed back unperturbed.

'When I yelled to bring attention to the fact that I was being robbed, those guys pointed at me and yelled, '*Pocketmaar*' and ......and pointed at me and assaulted me. ME. THOSE MADARCHOTS. They robbed me and turned around and pointed the finger at me.'

Some of the young men at the street corner brazenly laughed at this.

'I was on my way to pay my exam fees. It is the last day. If I don't make it I lose six months.' Anand was now tearful. The crowd began to disperse. There seemed to be no resolution in sight. Certainly there was no action or excitement.

Rashid walked over to the gaggle of guys. '*Bhaiyo*, I am from your *mohalla*.' He began and then cleared his throat nervously before going on. 'That guy there is a doctor. A good, kind man. He takes care of my family when I take them in to the hospital. He probably takes care of your families too. And how do we repay him? By robbing him. Robbing him so that he can't take his exams. Can't do what he does selflessly. Can't take care of us!' Rashid was surprised by his own eloquence.

Apparently he had struck a chord. The ruffians were silent. One of them beckoned him.

'How much money was there?' Rashid turned to Anand who promptly replied.

'Four hundred rupees.'

The hood, obviously in some leadership position amongst the gathered youth scratched his neck and very deliberately pulled out a wad of notes. He peeled off four hundred rupee notes and handed them to Rashid. Rashid pushed them into Anand's hand.

'And my wallet...' Anand began. Rashid shushed him, leading him away.

'Forget about that. Here's some change for the bus. I'll wait with you till you get on.'

After that episode Rashid often met Anand in the hospital. They exchanged pleasantries and some personal news. Anand learnt that Rashid had quit college and was working in the leather business. Rashid sought him out when he needed a family member taken care of.

Late one night he saw Anand and Soma at a *lassi* stall. It was 2 am and he was walking home from a friend's house. Once again Hindu-Muslim sibling rivalry had taken an ugly turn. The communal conflagration had claimed many lives, yet he felt secure. The locality was predominantly Muslim and he knew almost everyone. The city was still seething from the outpouring of violence.

Soma swayed slightly and Anand looked uncomfortable. Curiosity piqued Rashid walked over to them.

'Hello. Late night?' Rashid queried. Anand looked up and smiled.

'I was reading for a test.' He looked over to Soma who was looking at her feet trying to steady herself. She lurched forward and her foot splashed some flowing effluent in the open drain outside the shop. Anand tightened his grip on her arm.

'Her idea. She had to have some *jalebis*. She was out at some party and just got back. I tried to reason with her but....'

The other clientele at the shop was now increasingly interested in the drunk girl. One of them leerily said, 'She needs some of my special treatment. She will get sober instantly. Probably gave her *chutiya* to some rich kid with a small prick. Fucking Hindu slut.'

Anand looked around worriedly, a bit out of his depth. The *thelawalla* handed a hot packet of greasy *jalebis* double wrapped in newspaper. The trio turned around to walk away. Their path was blocked. No one stepped aside. Rashid looked up. There was no one he recognized.

'Do you guys know Altaf? I am his friend, Rashid,' he started. 'This is my cousin and his friend. We don't want any trouble. Please let us pass.'

The leery man was not done.

'Your cousin,' he asked suspiciously. 'He looks like one of those medical students. He does not look Muslim.'

Rashid laughed out loud though his insides were quivering. He felt a nether loosening and his intestinal contents propelled downwards. Tightening his sphincter he looked his counterpart in the eye.

'So, Muslims can't be medical students? Is that some law? Now let us pass please.'

'Munirbhai kaheko panga karte ho. Lo lassi piyo. Abhi jaane do.' The

jalebiwala tried to keep the peace. Munir bhai felt the momentum slip and swaggered away. Rashid led his friends through.

'Let me walk you back to your campus.'

'You are always delivering me from these awful situations,' Anand gushed.

'I am sure you would do the same for me. I want to apologise for that man and his behaviour,' Rashid replied, looking at Anand gravely.

'You apologize. Why you? Just because he is Muslim? Are you and I only identified by our religion? I don't think so. Rogues will misbehave given the opportunity. And we have enough politicians that keep creating rifts. Hindus are equally bad if not worse.' They had reached the campus gates. Rashid stepped back. Anand turned around, his kind eyes crinkled into a smile. 'Thank you again.'

Soma leaned her head on his shoulder as he led her away.

After a few months Anand suddenly disappeared. Rashid went to the hospital a few times and looked around for him. He saw Soma, but she didn't seem to recognize him. In time he didn't see her around too. Rashid gradually forgot about them. Many, many years later he was walking to his car when he bumped into a man.

'Mangalya Dham, can you show me the way?'. 'That's where I live,' began Rashid. The kind eyes were bleary, puffed but still kind.

'Anand, Dr. Anand... ?' he asked.

'Yes,' Anand replied, 'But just Anand, never did become a bloody doctor. And you are...?'

'Rashid, remember me? Here get into my car. We can talk on the way home.'

He helped the intoxicated man into the passenger seat and started the car.

'Oh! You must be the new family that moved in. My son Rahim told me about it. Apparently, he has already had some interactions with your son... what name did he give...Arun?'

'Arjun,' Anand corrected. 'Someday I will fill in the gaps about my life. For now, you have again come through for me. You are like a guardian angel Rashid *bhai*. And the years have been kind.'

'*Inshallah*,' Rashid replied. 'I have my own leather shop now. My eldest son is in the Airforce. He flies fighter planes. Rahim is our baby. How is Soma? Or is it Soma *bhabhi*?'

A wistful look came over Anand's face.

'I have so much to tell you. Some other time….'

7

At the Quaid-E-Azam airport, Arjun groggily cleared the formalities and walked out wheeling a rickety, squeaky cart. His suitcase and kitbag tottered dangerously. Outside he peered around seeking a familiar face. An Indian official pushed his way through the crowd and greeted him.

'Comfortable flight sir? Myself Mr. Shah, give me bags. This is Munaf, Pakistan liaison for our team.' Munaf bowed a hasty greeting and lunged for the bags with a cheery, 'Welcome to Pakistan *saar*. I am friend of Rashid *bhai*. You knows him no?' Arjun shook his head in assent and relinquished his luggage. He shook the proffered hands and stepped in stride with the rapidly ambulating duo.

'Please call me Arjun. Yes, very comfortable, first time I have flown. Thanks for meeting me.' Mr. Shah did not break stride; replying while maneuvering the cart adroitly.

'No problem sir. This way sir...eh .Arjun.'

Munaf chimed in with an afterthought, 'Welcome to Karachi *saar*'. He hailed a cab bundled Arjun and the officious Mr. Shah in. He then went around the back and personally supervised the placement of the bags. Once he was content that the bags had been appropriately secured, he walked back and took his place next to the *paan* chewing driver. He turned and looked into the rear seat. 'We will be at the hotel soon, *saar* eh.'

Arjun looked out at the city whirring by him as the cab sped away. Karachi, the capital of the province of Sindh. The financial and political heart of the country. A city set on the Arabian Sea that was home to more than nine million. Affluent neighborhoods alternated with sprawling slums mainly

98

inhabited by refugees from Bangladesh, formerly East Pakistan. Mr. Shah was quiet during the entire trip.

The cab abruptly stopped in front of a large hotel. Mr. Shah jumped out to handle the luggage, pay the cabbie and sort out formalities with the hotel's front desk. He returned, 'Sir, I will take care of the bags. There is a team meeting on. They want you there, room 311. Okay sir.' He gazed up at Arjun and corrected himself. 'Alright, alright...Aaarjun'.

Arjun took the short elevator ride up and hesitantly knocked on the room door. He walked in to a raucous welcome. Cheers, catcalls and back slaps were bestowed on him by his teammates. Arjun shrugged shyly and sat down. The room settled and the discussion resumed. As the captain began outlining strategy for the upcoming game, Arjun felt a flush creep through him. All thoughts of sleep left his mind as he settled down to listen. The next game was the next day.

Thoughts crowded Arjun's mind. From the philosophical to the mundane to the downright inane. Arjun fought the lassitude that descended over him for a while, before the circling blackness of sleep engulfed him. Arjun slept well; a hectic last few days and the conviction that he would not be called up to play in the eleven, facilitated a dream free night.

The team bus ferried them to the stadium. The security arrangements for the trip were tremendous and had been beefed up even more in Karachi. Karachi had a volatile combination of Urdu speaking Muhajirs or refugees from India that had settled there after the partition in 1947 and native Sindhis. The city that grew by 400,000 each year had been a hotbed of continued sectarian, ethnic, political and economic unrest. In a glaring incident in 1986 *Pashtoons* descended from the Pirabad hills and attacked Biharis and Mujahirs. Munaf provided all of this information in an animated monologue.

'We are now driving by Clifton beach. Very posh area. In the evening you can come for camel ride. Our past leader Bhutto has house here. Number 70. His daughter Begum Benazir also stayed here, in Bilawal house,' Munaf droned on.

The captain sat beside Arjun on the trip. 'You're in Arjun,' he said nonchalantly, as they walked into the dressing room; barely suppressing a smile as Arjun's jaw dropped. 'It's do or die. Gotta play all my aces.'

Outside, the clouds had thickened casting a gloomy pall over the field. Mantri stepped out of the commentary booth and cast a wary look skywards as an isolated raindrop plinked on his face. Straightening his tie, he faced the camera.

'Welcome ladies and gentlemen. Another fine day, with a possibility of showers later on. A must win situation for India. A few team notes. Star batsman Suchen Chemburkar has undergone extensive testing including a MRI and has been cleared to play. The diagnosis is a nasty bruise. The little master continues to recuperate in Mumbai, however he has indicated his availability to return to the side if needed. India makes one change in the side. Young Mumbai middle order batsman Arjun makes his international debut bringing some much needed pizzazz to the line up. Azam has won the toss and elected to bat. Things are about to get underway, lets join the action on the field.'

The game began and it was another frustrating outing for the Indian bowlers. They were unable to bowl to a plan, seemingly confused between attack and containment. The swashbuckling Pakistani batsmen feasted on a surplus of short balls and long hops. Play paused momentarily as the Pakistani leader Pervez Musharraf took his place in the audience. At the crowds' urging he stepped out onto a balcony, looking up briefly as an errant raindrop found the tip of his nose. The skies he saw were the very same when he had circled in on October 12 1999, finally landing with only ten minutes of fuel remaining in his plane. His rapid ascension to power that followed, was now folklore. He shivered, possibly from the memory of that momentous day and returned into his bulletproof enclosure allowing the game to recommence. The allotted fifty overs came to an end. Pakistan had reached 301 for 6.

Wandrekar summed up the morning session, 'An absorbing morning of cricket. India again finds itself with its back to the wall. A masterful display of controlled aggression by the Pakistani batsmen. With storm clouds looming, India has to make sure they are equal to the task ahead and don't make heavy weather of the vaunted Pakistani pace attack. A few early breakthroughs and the hosts will be on their way to a watertight 3-0 lead in the five match series.' Wandrekar was obviously pleased with his own wit as he finished.

At that very moment, the Athavale family, Pranay, Rahim, Mrs. Gadkari and many other neighbors were gathered around in the Athavale drawing room glued to the television watching cricket. A TV camera had been set up at one side of the room; while in another corner, former India skipper Kapat Tej sat getting his make up adjusted. Kapat now hosted the most popular TV show dedicated to all things cricket. The technical crew rushed about getting ready for the shot. Kapat took his place and after a few hasty dabs at his face, signaled his readiness. The cameras rolled,

'Today on 'Opening spell,' we are spending a morning with the family of young Mumbai batsman Arjun who is making his debut for the country. As you can see a lot of well-wishers have gathered to watch him make his debut. The game has stopped for lunch; we will take this opportunity to chat with a few people.'

Kapat hopped down from his perch and almost ran into Mrs. Athavale who was hurrying around with a tray of food. 'You must be really proud today right?'

Mrs. Athavale set down the tray. 'I only hope he is eating well. He has never spent so much time away. You know. Alone. By himself.'

Kapat turned to a hovering Pallavi. 'What are Arjun's strengths as a batsman?'

'His batting of course. He is strong on both sides of the wicket.' Pallavi launched into a detailed analysis of Arjun's technique; finishing with, 'The only problem is against a left arm spinner coming round the wicket...oops maybe I should not say that.' Pallavi cupped her hands over her mouth and charged away.

Kapat turned to Rahim, 'I am told that you are the arch enemy of Arjun on the cricket field. *Jaise kehte hain na, kattar dushman.* So are you praying for an early dismissal?'

Rahim shook his head vehemently, 'Of course not. Now it is a matter of national pride. Mark my words, Arjun will smash those Paki bowlers. I have prepared him well.'

Mrs. Gadkari shoved Rahim aside and barged into the frame. Kapat sized her up and asked, 'Any recollections of Arjun's growing years?' The feisty widow adjusted her sari and glared at the camera. 'In our society we have always been very supportive. Why my dear departed husband Mr. Gadkari, may his soul rest in everlasting peace always said, 'That boy will go far'.' With this she cast a wistful look at her news papered windows. 'I have many mementos of his dashing strokes.'

Kapat next walked up to Pranay who had been waiting patiently beside Mrs. Gadkari. 'You have been his teammate and even his captain. Any insights?' Pranay had a sagacious look on his face. He chose his words carefully. 'As long as he keeps focused and concentrates, the sky is the limit.'

Kapat walked over to Arjun's father who hid behind a newspaper. Kapat peered over the paper and asked, 'Any words of advice for your son?'

Mr. Athavale set the paper down and reached for his foaming mug of beer. He carefully folded his glasses. 'The boy needs self-confidence. A belief in his abilities both as a cricketer and as a human being. If he can harness that inner strength and belief, success will be his.'

The director frantically pointed to his watch asking Kapat to wrap it up.

'There you have it. Concern, confidence, advice and above all heartfelt good wishes to Arjun from his near and dear. That's all for now. Thank you for joining me on a special mid-match edition of 'Opening spell',' Kapat concluded.

Wandrekar welcomed viewers back to the post lunch session.

'Welcome back. The Indian openers are making their way out for what promises to be an interesting duel.'

The Indian openers started purposefully; lashing out at everything; trying to get ahead of the required rate while the fielding restrictions were in place. But the bowlers pegged away and finally chances started going to hand. At the 25 over mark India were 130 for 5. As Arjun walked out to bat it began to rain. The players waited briefly but as the precipitation intensified they left the field as the grounds crew rushed out with the covers. The downpour looked menacing but abruptly petered out. The covers were dragged off and the sun even peered out from behind the still turgid clouds. Play was set to commence.

Mantri welcomed the patient television audience back. 'The covers are off. The teams are making their way back onto the field. Due to the stoppage the Duckworth-Lewis rule has come into play. The Indian innings has been reduced to 35 overs and they will face a revised target of 212 for victory. A tall task with not much batting to follow.'

The Indian batsmen stepped out. The magnitude of the task was not lost on them. The opening bat who still survived was in thunderous form and smacked the bowling all over the field.

With 25 runs to get from 2 overs the marauding opener was bowled. The next man walked in with instructions for Arjun to take over. He nudged a single of the first ball bringing Arjun back on strike. Arjun picked up runs, driving through gaps and hitting over the infield. Yet with 17 runs to get off the last 4 balls not many gave India even an outside chance. Arjun had a steely look on his face as he reverse swept the left arm spinner for two fours and top edged the next ball over the keeper for four more.

Five runs were needed of the last ball. The field spread out. The spinner saw Arjun step out and dug a short ball into the ribs. Arjun rocked back and hooked it away. The ball flew high but fell short of fine leg. Just two. Arjun's family and all those gathered with them around the television groaned. The groan quickly changed into a cheer as the camera swung over to the umpire, who signaled a no ball. The left-armer had stepped over in his hurry to deliver the ball.

Arjun took a moment to settle down as Azam adjusted the field around. The next ball was fuller. Arjun drove and the ball bounced off the hand of the fielder at short cover. The batsmen were through for one and with little to lose charged back for the second. Short cover compounded his earlier error by fumbling slightly before unleashing a missile that disrupted the stumps with a direct hit. The third umpire was called to duty.

The silence in the Athavale living room was deafening. Pallavi covered her eyes while Pranay started on the dead skin around his bitten fingernails.

NOT OUT.

Arjun was delirious and ran back with his signature pumping of fists. The other batsman stopped to pick up a souvenir stump. It was a memorable win. The Athavale living room exploded. Mrs. Gadkari raised her hands and attempted to jump on her arthritic knees; in the process upsetting the plateful of food resting in her lap.

An obviously elated Wandrekar spouted superlatives. 'A glorious victory. Superb batting from the openers. Innovative strokes from debutant Arjun; intervention from the weather gods and a healthy slice of luck see India through. India lives to battle another day and we will bring you all the action on Saturday. Till then goodbye!'

The replays played repeatedly after the game showed the no-ball call to be marginal. That and the botched pick up on the last ball that was instrumental in allowing Arjun to make his ground, led more than one viewer to chalk this victory up to divine intervention.

8

The players trooped off the bus, a tired but happy lot. As they stood by the elevators the captain turned and addressed them.

'Now guys, listen up! No team meeting tonight. Some of us are coming down to the coffee shop to get a bite. Anyone that wants to join us is welcome?' Arjun stood and looked around, not wanting to be the first to answer. His roommate Nakul quickly said, 'No! It's been a long day. I think I'll get room service and curl up with a book.'

The captain looked inquiringly at Arjun,

'How about you kid?' Arjun was caught in two minds. The novelty of being a part of the national side had not worn out. He wanted to experience all he could. Yet felt as though he may be letting his roommate down by venturing out late.

'Uh! Oh! OK.'

He murmured indecisively glancing at Nakul, who signaled approval with a slight nod. The captain reclaimed Arjun's attention.

'Eight o'clock then, in the lobby.'

Exactly as the huge grandfather clock in the lobby struck eight a spic and span, spruced up Arjun walked out and joined his waiting captain. The skipper gave a low whistle, 'The damsels better watch out. You clean up well.'

Arjun shrugged uncomfortably as a few other players joined them and the happy horde fell into formation like dutiful lemmings behind their skipper and sauntered across to the coffee shop. Just as they were about to walk in, a small boy detached himself from his parents and ran up to them, 'Autograph please.'

The skipper held out his hand with the air of one who was familiar with the drill. The little boy withdrew the extended book and clutched it close to his chest, 'Not you.' He said and shyly pointed to Arjun, 'Him!'

Arjun gingerly took the book, scrawled his name and handed it back with a smile. The captain was not one to let any opportunity for leg-pulling go by.

'*Wah beta*! Just one game and already a hero. You have arrived kid! Enjoy the ride.'

The interior of the coffee shop was dimly lit and smoky; this was one of the happening places in the city. Airline crews mingled with businessmen seeking a kindred spirit, miles away from home. In this Islamic country this was one of the places a non-Muslim could get alcoholic drinks and some locals were furtively checking out if they could score a few. A crowd was gathered at one end of a long bar. Intermittent bawdy laughter erupted. About a quarter of the other tables were occupied.

The cricketers looked around for a few empty tables together and spotting a cluster of tables close to the bar they spread out, occupying three tables. Arjun slid into a seat on the last table. He looked around at the rambunctious cacophony, unsure as to what he should do next.

The lanky pacer sprawled lazily in the seat next to him inquired, 'What will you have?'

Arjun fidgeted uncomfortably. 'Coca cola' he replied hesitantly; hurriedly adding, 'Without ice'.

The pacer relayed the order to the bartender. There was a flurry of activity behind the bar and soon drinks were served. The skipper reached for his wallet and came up empty. The team erupted in laughter and the captain looked around sheepishly. As a couple of the other players reached for their wallets he waved them aside and stood up and looked directly at Arjun.

'Be right back. Just going to run up to my room and pick up my wallet.'

Arjun smiled, 'All right.'

As the captain left, conversation picked up at the table. The lanky speedster demonstrated how he had set up one of the star Pakistani batsmen. The players clustered around the adjacent table. Arjun tried to get a look in, but could not penetrate the tight knit group.

He settled back into his chair and turned his attention back to his Coke. He looked around and noticed he had company. He was sandwiched between two women who had pulled up chairs next to him. The smell of perfume was overwhelming. He was almost thankful when one of them blew smoke in his face. Uncertain as to how he should handle this situation, Arjun initially assiduously avoided eye contact. He concentrated on the popping bubbles in his coke. Finally unable to resist, he darted stealthy glances in their direction under hooded eyes. Various bits of bulging anatomy were thrust in his direction, barely covered by fit-to-bust clothes. Arjun tried to shrink into his chair, blend into the upholstery. Apparently he was unsuccessful, as the brassy obviously dyed blonde to his right leaned over,

'Hey! What have we here? Lost your mama?'

The dark haired one to the left uncrossed her legs, all *faux naïve*. 'Out so late on a school night.'

Arjun was decidedly uncomfortable and stammered something unintelligible. The blonde put a hand on his shoulder, 'You look cold. Nothing like somebody hot to warm you up.' She perched herself on the armrest of Arjun's chair. Arjun shifted away. The second woman thrust her drink in his face, 'Here, have a sip. Won't feel cold then. Have a few and you won't feel much of anything.'

At this witticism, both women threw their heads back and laughed. Arjun tried to get up. The girls playfully pushed him down. Arjun flailed, suddenly an authoritative voice cut in.

'That's enough. I think the boy wants to get up.'

Nakul stood glaring at the two women, Munaf was hovering behind him. Nakul held out a hand to Arjun and hauled him up.

'Just having some fun.'

'Yeah, no harm just fun', the girls offered by way of explanation. The girls drifted away, weakly adding, 'Why don't you join us too, big boy?'

The withering look from Nakul was an ample answer. The scene drew attention from the rest of the crowd and the Indian players crowded around curious about the fracas. Nakul turned to them. His voice had a steely edge.

'Nice work guys. Way to look out for the kid.' Putting his arm around Arjun, he continued, 'Hey Arjun, you OK, can I get you something?'

Arjun was near tears. He mumbled, 'No, nothing! Can we just leave? I want to go back.'

'Of course, let's go.' Nakul kept his arm on Arjun's shoulder and led him to the door; Munaf followed half a step behind. They almost bumped into the skipper; charging back with his wallet clutched victoriously in his hand.

Watching his departing teammates he ventured, 'Everything all right?'

Nakul looked up, 'No. It isn't. Not really,' and walked on with Arjun without any further explanation. The skipper shrugged and walked in to join the other players who filled him in with their version of the happenings. Munaf caught up with the duo in the lobby.

'I knows those two. They are up to no good. Good you comes there *saar*,' he obsequiously addressed Nakul.

Nakul waved him away, 'Thanks, thanks for everything Munaf.'

Nakul snapped the light on in their room and sprawled out on his bed dangling his shoes over the edge. He flipped on the TV and skipped through the channels a few times, his brow knotted. Arjun sat on the edge of his bed with his hands clenched nervously. Nakul looked up abruptly,

'No need to get upset. They wouldn't have done anything. You need to learn to stand your ground. Speak up. Don't get cornered and don't be ashamed of being young, naïve or anything. If you do not, there are all kinds of people out there waiting to take advantage. Understand!'

Arjun was taken aback by this outburst, but looked up to see compassionate and concerned eyes observing him. He concurred demurely, 'Understand.' Nakul continued, 'Now you haven't eaten anything. Let's get some room service.'

Arjun settled down on his bed and by the time Nakul finished ordering a club sandwich and some hot chocolate the relieved boy was fast asleep. Nakul called to cancel the order and turned out the light.

While the players slept, the airwaves were buzzing. The next morning, all the leading dailies in Mumbai carried the picture. Arjun had a rather beatific smile on his face looking deliriously happy; flanked by the two girls. His father put the paper down with a 'Bah' for effect. The headline, 'ARJUN SPREADS WINGS,' stared back at him. He turned around and addressed any and all that cared to listen, 'It didn't take him long to go back to his loafer ways.'

Jumping to her son's defense Mrs. Athavale attempted to assuage, 'I am sure there is a reasonable explanation. My Arjun would not.'

The roar that erupted from her husband's mouth startled her, 'What explanation can there be?' He waved the newspaper for effect. 'Everything is crystal clear. That boy sure knows how to get in the midst of controversy.'

His wife tut-tutted and made soothing gestures. 'Now don't get worked up. The doctor has said it's bad for your blood pressure. You will start those scary chest pains again. We will clear everything when he comes back. In the meantime let me call that Singhji at CBA.'

'BCA,' Mr. Athavale snorted, 'What good is that?' He turned to the wide-eyed Pallavi who comprehending that something serious was going on, had distanced herself from the scene.

'Here Pallu, call his hotel number. I want to have a talk with him right now.'

Mr. Athavale stopped speaking abruptly. His body heaved as he coughed. The entire episode was capped with a violent upchuck, the vomitus on the floor was blood red. Pallavi and her mother looked at each other agitatedly. Mr. Athavale silenced them before they could speak by raising his hand and waving them away.

There was a five day break between the third and fourth matches. Most of the team was staying put in Karachi for a few days before moving on to Lahore. Nakul and Sainath had planned a few days of sightseeing. Munaf had arranged for it all and they were to leave after breakfast for a day trip to Mohenjodaro; the breathtaking site of an ancient Indus valley civilization.

At breakfast the next morning, Arjun's dog like devotion to Nakul and his obvious despondency at his impending departure did not escape the captain's eye. The captain had intended to keep Arjun with the team but in a gesture driven by the impetuousness and sudden insight that had characterized his people skills driven, sometimes brilliant captaincy; he pulled Nakul aside and asked if he would take Arjun along with him. Nakul studied his skipper's serious face and agreed. A quick check with Munaf revealed that it would be no big deal to add Arjun to the sightseeing party. The captain broke the news to Arjun who could barely mask his excitement, but guiltily kept seeking reassurance that it would be okay, till his smiling skipper shooed him away.

The touring party was assigned a small security detail. Irfan, Imran, Aslam and Asif looked alike. Their laconic exteriors and saturnine features appeared to have been created from the same mould. Munaf and the three cricketers were bundled into the middle row of a capacious van while the muscled foursome divided themselves between the front and rear seats. Munaf resumed his monotonous drone as they set off. He was a treasure trove of information with an amazing capacity for continuous speech.

'We are now passing the mausoleum of Qaid-E-Azam Jinnah, the founder of Pakistan. Everyday a lot of people gather here to watch the changing of the guard.' Munaf pointed out of the slightly grimy windows. Arjun dozed for most of the hair-raising drive which took half the day.

After a quick lunch they set out to explore Mohenjodaro one of the seats of the amazing 2000 BC Indus valley civilization. Mohenjodaro literally meant 'mound of the dead.' A local guide pointed out the architectural finds. Arjun wandered through the carefully excavated city where a main street, public sewers, organized dwelling, public baths and a writing system had been identified. There was no evidence of any organized religion. No palaces or temples had come to light. Government buildings had been anticipated, but none had been found and further excavation was going to be close to impossible with the rising ground water level. Lost in the sea of baked clay bricks Arjun came face to face with his own insignificance. The past few months had seemed to revolve around him. First he had scarcely believed his peripeteia. Being thrust into the limelight had bolstered his ego, but also edged his awareness with a heightened sense of expectation. Arjun suddenly felt at peace. His concerns coalesced into a sense of complacency. The furiously spinning puzzle pieces in his brain slowed down. A pattern seemed discernable. It would all happen. Unfettered by what he did, what had to happen would happen. His actions at best could shape a moment, an hour, a day, but creation would chart it's own course and march on relentlessly; notwithstanding whether he succeeded or failed.

Arjun looked around to see if these weighty thoughts had occurred to others in his party. Nakul and Sainath were embroiled in an argument about the merits or lack thereof of the new Pakistani left arm spin sensation, Wazir Khan. Munaf had disappeared as he was prone to and the hovering musclemen, clad in crisp polyester, hid their feelings behind identical Ray-bans.

Arjun savored his personal enlightenment, with a stray thought; maybe Buddha felt the same under the Bodhisattva. The return journey to their hotel was subdued. Arjun steadfastly gazed out of the window, biting his upper lip, as thoughts and emotions pinged inside his confined calvarium like a crazed computer game.

The tired trio retired early. In the darkened hotel room, the shrill trill of the telephone knifed through the darkness. Arjun arose and sleepily moved to answer it. Nakul bounded up and gestured him away. He deliberately picked up the instrument and ventured a guarded, 'Hello!' A look of relief crossed his visage as he scratched his head absent-mindedly, 'Hello? Yes… Yes… We are in another hotel now. Yes, I will give you my cell; you can reach Arjun on it anytime. Just a minute.'

Nakul covered the mouthpiece and whispered, 'It's your father.'

Arjun took the phone nervously. 'Hello *baba*. Yes…No, that's not what happened…. I wasn't drinking.. No …You've got it all wrong.'

The yelling at the other end of the line filled the room. Arjun shifted uncomfortably and for the second time in two nights, he looked close to tears. Nakul put a finger on his lips and asked for the phone; Arjun handed it to him. Seizing an opening in the diatribe, likely when Arjun's father stopped to take a breath; Nakul interjected, the words poured out.

'This is Nakul again. Yes. Let me explain. Arjun was just out with the boys for some food when these two girls sort of forcibly started a conversation with him. He just didn't know how to extricate himself. Yes … of course. We are all taking care of him. No.. Don't worry. Yes. Thank you.' He concluded and handed the phone back to Arjun.

The tone at the other end was now decidedly more placatory. 'OK *baba*! … Yes I will. Bye.'

Arjun put the phone down. Nakul had one more firm lesson to deliver before the boys settled back in bed.

'And one more thing. Be very careful when you answer the phone, all kinds of people call up. Make sure you know the person at the other end before having any kind of conversation.'

A sleepy Arjun nodded agreement. The excitement was catching up with him and he lay back to snatch a few more hours of slumber.

The next morning the three cricketers rose early and boarded a puddle jumper to Quetta the capital of the vast under populated, inaccessible and remote Baluchistan. The Chagai hills lay to their west, the site of Pakistan's nuclear explosions; which had raised justifiable fears of an escalating arms race in the subcontinent. A popular saying claimed that the creator, after creating the world threw the leftovers in Baluchistan. A brooding melancholy prevailed over the entire city. Unseasonal rain drove the avid sightseers back to the hotel. A let-up in the downpour saw the stir-crazy trio in the parking lot; limbering up, stretching and performing calisthenics. Munaf had stepped out and returned with the news that he had procured an earlier flight to Peshawar. Speeding through the narrow lanes of Quetta the visitors were left with a lasting memory of the smuggler's bazaar and the unyielding dreariness of the city.

9

 Arjun's heroics had not gone unnoticed. He was an overnight heartthrob and many a nubile nymphet professed a strong desire to mother him. Pallavi took all this in, incredulous that her dweeby brother could inspire such passion. She turned on the television. Rani Ramani, the latest fast-talking, much pierced video jockey was conducting some street interviews. The editing was deliberately choppy. The camera zoomed and panned dizzily. Rani's high-pitched breathless expounding assaulted the senses.

'On this segment of Spicy Cricket we are going to the streets to find out whether people think India can win the next two ODIs.' She thrust the microphone at a startled passer-by.

'What do you think?'

The young man recovered well, 'Of course India will win. We have strong batting.' He grabbed the mike back to add, 'And Santoshi ma is on our side.'

Rani made google eyes at the camera and turned to a man who had till that moment been engaged in slow sidle designed to get him into the frame.

'What do you think?' The second man was nonplussed for a bit and tried a reverse sidling maneuver. His friend gustily stated the obvious, 'With Suchen anything is possible.'

'But Suchen is injured.' Rani countered.

'Then no guarantee' was the prompt reply. Rani changed directions, 'Achcha! Who is your favorite?'

The replies came fast and furious, 'Suchen', 'Suchen', 'Nakul', 'Rangoli'. Rani spied a gaggle of giggling girls in the background and motioned to them. She walked over as they stepped forward shyly, nudging each other nervously. Rani waved the mike before them and asked, 'Girls, who is your favorite cricketer.' The girls gave this some thought and the first said, 'Nakul.'

Her friend grabbed the mike and blurted, 'Arjun'.

Rani attempted a befuddled look, 'Achcha! Arjun. Why? He hasn't played much'.

The excited collegian gushed, 'He is just cho chweet.'

Pallavi stuck her fingers deep into her mouth and made puky sounds, as Rani echoed,

'Cho chweet! How about you?' She turned to the third girl.

'Arjun!' she said, coyly.

One of her friends in the background, fearing that she would not be polled, felt compelled to yell, 'Suchen! All the way..'

Pallavi darted up to switch channels as Rani concluded.

'There you have it. There is now a new entrant into the ranks of cricketer heartthrobs. Till next time this is..'

Pallavi switched the set off.

Arjun woke up refreshed in Peshawar, the winter residence of the Afghan kings. On the way over, Munaf had been the usual infallible and garrulous source of information. Arjun had actually tuned into his incessant chatter and now knew that Pakistan which was set up as a utopian Islamic state, literally meant, 'land of the pure.' The sixty year old military nation, the only one besides Israel created in the name of religion, had a chequered history, marred by political instability and deep seated economic and social problems. Language, ethnicity, sect and tribe divided its four disparate provinces. Peshawar, a dusty border town near the Khyber Pass exuded a rugged and lawless aura. Pastel villas alternated with *madarasas*. Ever so often, the tinny voices of the muezzins called the faithful to prayer. Burkha-clad women flitted around, the shrouded eyes saw all. Weapons were everywhere.

'There are 7 millions Kalashnikovs in the frontier province.' Munaf proclaimed.

'This, in the land of Khan Abdul Gaffar Khan, the frontier Gandhi,' remarked Nakul, his voice laced with irony.

Exquisite Mughal architecture and nomadic tent colonies were all around. As they drove by the 17th century Mahabad Khan mosque, the faithful washed themselves outside the building before stepping in to pray. Qisa Khawani or the storyteller's bazaar was deserted. Munaf informed them that traveling salesmen gathered there each evening and exchanged anecdotes and experiences over tea.

That afternoon they set off along the Karakoram highway. The highest highway in the world was built over a twenty-year span. It ran along the Indus, along the ancient Silk route to China. This was Munaf's special treat. The proximity to Kashmir meant that the presence of Indians would be less than welcome, yet there was so much to see. Their van was sandwiched between extravagantly decorated trucks that plodded onward in an unlikely bridal procession amid the bleak mountainous desert which lay around them.

That evening they halted in Karimabad in the Hunza valley. The little hamlet was autonomously ruled by its own mayor till 1974. It was settled by Ismailis, a 7th century sect which looked upto the westernized Aga Khan as their spiritual leader. The province had merited mention in Kipling's "Kim" and was a popular trekkers and mountaineering destination. The towering peaks of K2 and Nanga Parbat beckoned adventurers relentlessly.

The next day they took in the massive Gandhara Buddha sculptures. The normally placid enlightened one displayed a veneer of arrogance. Late in the day they found their way to Taxila. The early evening sun cast a warm glow over the ruins that stretched over 15 square miles. The tranquility exuded by the ruins was contagious. The entourage drifted into the museum, the displays emanated serenity, elegance and an easy sensuality. They walked by the monastery of Julian, named after a Roman envoy who converted to Buddhism. The saffron-clad monks drifting between the ruins had an aura of austerity and pacifism.

Arjun looked at them and the epiphany that had started in Mohenjodaro gathered momentum. The pieces shifted and rearranged in his mind. The picture was less hazy.

'How easy, it could be! How easy it is, if we all learnt to tolerate, to leave and let live.' The infectious peace of his environs entered him and he thought back to his algebra equations. *Quod erat demonstrandum*, his mind said.

Thus it is proved. This is how it should be, quite easily done.

That evening Sainath showed him a cartoon from the newspaper. It showed a forward thinking sprinter donning Pakistan colours ready to sprint into the future; while a bearded mullah next to him looked back in time. That captured the essence of Pakistan's decision. How forward thinking would they be? How mired in the past? Setting serious thoughts aside Arjun traveled to Islamabad with a light heart. He had a game to play.

The fourth game and all the usual suspects were gathered around the television. A bright and well-scrubbed Rabi Mantri greeted them.

'Good morning all! The crucial fourth one-day international between India and Pakistan is about to begin. Azam has won the toss and elected to field. India has chosen to retain the side that won the last ODI, Pakistan makes one....'

The game began; the Indian openers seized the initiative early with some bold and creative hitting. The scoreboard hummed like a contented well-oiled machine. Arjun got his chance to bat in the slog overs. He started cautiously, nervously fingering his gloves but soon settled in to grab quick ones and twos with the occasional hit to the fence.

Wazir Khan, the left arm spinner signaled to the umpire that he was coming around the wicket.

'He's got him!,' Pallavi exclaimed confidently.

'Shut up, you *panvati*,' yelled Pranay.

'Just watch,' retorted Pallavi.

The next ball was dug in a bit short. Arjun rocked back and tried to pull it. The ball ballooned up to midwicket who pocketed it gleefully. Mantri stated the obvious.

'Forty five useful runs.'

'Which runs are not useful,' Pallavi queried.

'That was not a good stroke,' Mantri continued.

'He got out, didn't he?' Pranay parried, throwing a cushion at the television.

Unaware of how incendiary his innocuous comments were in the Athavale household, Mantri concluded, 'A promising innings comes to an end.'

'Abbe chup saale', shouted Rahim, as the children walked away from the

television; their interest somewhat dampened.

'I told him to avoid that stroke. He hits that against the turn. Does anyone listen to me?' Pallavi wailed.

Mrs. Gadkari got up and picked up some of the food laid out. She walked over to the kids, 'Now what? We will probably lose.'

Mr. Athavale felt obliged to explain the nuances of the game, 'Not so quick! As the great Lala said, 'Cricket is a game of.....'

The entire assembled populace chimed in, '...glorious uncertainties.'

The game had resumed and India reached 224 for 9, thanks to some lusty hitting by the tail-enders. Pakistan started batting and after a great start, lost wickets regularly. The lanky speedster was in a zone, striking early and often. The corridor outside the off stump was his and he was there with varied pace, swing and bounce. The Pakis never really recovered and the speedster's celebratory dance, a variation of the *bhangra* was seen repeatedly on TV screens across India. As the last wicket fell the entire congregation at the Athavale house rose as one and did their best rendition of the variant *bhangra*; along with '*balle balles*' of delight.

No one noticed Arjun's father sliding to the floor and when they did most felt that he was adding a variation of his own. Mr. Athavale clutched his chest and sucked valiantly for air which suddenly seemed rare. His cheeks puffed out and a torrent of blood poured onto the glistening floor. He crumpled over in his blood. Arjun's mother screamed and rushed to his side. Rahim and Pranay rushed out and a flood of neighbours poured in. Soon Mr. Athavale with tubes and devices trailing him like a *noveau royale* train bundled into the back of an ambulance. The neighborhood gathered to watch, drawn to tragedy as moths to a flame. Mrs. Gadkari consoled the weeping wife and escorted her to a waiting taxicab. Pallavi, in turn pleaded to be taken along. Mrs. Gadkari helped Jyoti Athavale into the taxi and got in after her. Jyoti leaned out and said tearfully, 'Pallu, call Savitri *kaki* and ask her to come over.' The small group watched the ambulance and cab leave the building, morbidly fascinated.

10

The tired cricketers trooped into the dressing room. The series was squared and the lanky speedster clutched his 'man of the match' trophy.

Sujay Wandrekar was summing up the game. 'Another absorbing duel. It seemed that all was lost until that jaw-dropping inspired spell.'

The speedster preened and took an impromptu bow.

'Aided by spectacular catching by a rejuvenated Indian side,' Wandrekar continued, 'It now comes down to the final game.' Wandrekar then looked down at a piece of paper just handed to him. 'We have a bit of sad news to report. Arjun Athavale's father was taken ill during the game and may need an emergent procedure or surgery. We have no other details at the moment.' A hushed silence spread across the dressing room like a shadow from a dense cloud. 'We do not yet know if Arjun will fly back. As you all know, Suchen, of his own accord will be flying out this evening, he will be available if needed.'

'That was tactful.' Nakul was the first to react flicking the set off and moving to Arjun's side. "Nothing like getting bad news through the TV.'

The dumbstruck youngster sat shocked. The unexpected news was too new and too fresh to educe a reaction. Nakul gently led him away.

The darkened room reflected the air of melancholy that prevailed. Nakul parted the drapes to let a sliver of light in. Arjun looked up stricken. He was holding the telephone. His knuckles were strained white. His shoulders were slumped with futility and frustration. His face was crisscrossed with tears that had been rubbed this way and that.

'I wonder why no one answers? They can't all be at the hospital. Was Wandrekar able to find out which hospital they took him to? Since he seems the first to know everything!' Arjun paused. Nakul walked over and put a comforting hand on his shoulder. The lanky speedster uncurled himself out of the lounger and straightened various bits of toiletry and pieces of paper scattered on the adjacent table. The jangle of the phone elicited a startled gasp from the frazzled nerves in the room. Nakul reached out and grabbed the phone.

'Hello. Yes, please hold. And our entire team is praying for a smooth recovery'.

He handed the instrument to Arjun who fumbled it in his eagerness to reach for it.

His voice was tearful and strained,'H..h..Hello!.' Unable to contain himself, he burst into tears. Valiantly attempting to regain composure he continued, 'How are you Baba? I will leave right away and come back.'

A pause as he listened, his eyes darted from left to right nervously and repeatedly. 'No I can't stay here and wonder what's happening there.'

At the other end the omnipresent antiseptic milieu bestowed an unreal calmness. Mr. Athavale raised himself slightly from his bed and tried to inject strength into his quavering voice.

'*Bachcha*, we all have to do what we are destined to. Your coming here will not change anything. I am in good hands here. Actually if you do come, it would upset me more. Stay there and complete your job. Give it your best...'. The effort of that monologue sapped the ailing man. He lay back and handed the small cell phone to his wife.

'How can I?' Arjun pleaded, 'I can't think of anything else.'

His mother's voice came back at him, instructing and expecting compliance, 'Your father needs to rest. We will call you as soon as the surgery is done. Stay there, do what you do best. Your doing that, will give us strength. Gadkari *aji* is with us. She will keep me company and help me through this.. Savitri *kaki* is home with Pallu.'

The tormented youth managed a reluctant and strained, 'All right, bye! Take care of him, *Aai*.' He gently put the phone down and it seemed like it was an eternity before he looked up. 'He wants me to stay and play.'

'You must do what you think is right. If you want to go we can surely make the arrangements,' offered Nakul. He was not saying anything Arjun didn't already know. But the repetition did underline the decision that had to be made.

Arjun straightened up and decisively steeled himself. 'I'll stay. I don't want to, but I will.' The resolution in his voice defused the tension. The speedster managed some nervous laughter while Nakul raised his hand with a thumbs-up sign, 'There you go.'

The real life drama surrounding the game did not escape attention in other parts of the media. That evening, Shankhar Subhash who fancied himself to be a bit of a shock jock couldn't resist a jab in his monologue.

'Now Suchen has decided to rejoin the team. I say don't. They have just started winning, why mess with something that's working. Just joking Suchen! You know of course, *Sare jahan se achcha hai Suchen hamara*. On a more serious note; all of our…. why just us, the nation's good wishes are with Mr. Athavale, Arjun's father. We wish him a successful surgery and a speedy recovery.'

The competing television station had an aging starlet playing vixen on her show titled, 'Anju, *kabhi garam kabhi naram*'. That evening on her show she batted her heavily mascaraed, false lashes.

'And a big *garam garam* to the in-form batting sensation… Arjun. Despite his father's illness he has decided to stay back in Pakistan for the final game. *Kya* dedication *yaar*! Some of our senior cricketers could learn from the youngster.'

The unfolding drama had captured a nation's attention. The young man in the middle of the maelstrom was blissfully unaware as he sat pensively in his room. His unseeing eyes were riveted on the flickering television image before him.

The doctor tried his best to explain in lay terms. Mr. Athavale was propped up in bed. A big tube entered through his nose, a balloon on its inner end was compressing the bleeding site in his gut, trying to stem the flow. Like a finger in the dyke. Blood dripped into him through an intravenous line.

'You had a small heart attack but that is all stable. Because of the bleeding, you were anemic. If we could stop the bleeding…. no more concern.'

'But why is it bleeding doctor?' Mrs. Athavale queried. Weighing his words to find a delicate way of explaining, the doctor settled for straight talk.

'You have a drinking problem right?'

Mr. Athavale nodded in assent. Denial was a thing of the past. ' I understand whats going on. Just explain to my wife', he said weakly.

'That causes your liver to harden up. Blood vessels bringing nutrients for further processing, face an increased pressure to enter the liver and choose other ways to bypass it. This leads to flimsy blood vessels with thin walls carrying an unusually large amount of blood. Sometimes the walls give way and blood pours out. Usually we are able to put an endoscope down your mouth and stop the hemorrhage. But in your case the bleeding vessel is recalcitrant.'

'What are the options?' Mrs. Athavale asked, unsure about whether she wanted that question answered.

'I'm glad we got to that. I am here to talk to you about it. Basically there are two things we could do.'

The doctor now slipped into a comfortably 'canned' speech. 'We could create a bypass or shunt for the blood; surgically. To divert blood away from the diseased liver through an artificial, more robust route. Unfortunately that procedure has high mortality if performed in the presence of acute bleeding; up to a 50% chance of dying.'

The physician paused gesturing towards the recumbent patient. He was at the end of his spiel; which seemed to energize him into going on. 'Luckily, we have another option. A radiologist colleague of mine has just returned from the US and is capable of creating such a shunt without surgery.'

The conversation was veering close to incomprehensible and Mrs. Athavale verbalized the obvious, 'but how'?

'He uses X-rays to see his way through veins and then puts a small tube to connect two veins in the liver, bypassing the hardened substance!' The doctor concluded triumphantly and stepped outside the room, returning with a diminutive, distinguished well-dressed young man. 'This is the doctor I was referring to; Dr. Patel. He has done many of these and I feel that it is imperative that we proceed soon. We are fighting a losing battle. He is losing more blood than we can replace and another massive episode could result in exsanguination.'

Mr. Athavale gestured helplessness. He wanted someone else to take the decision. This was all new since those hazy days in medical college.

Jyoti Athavale looked over to Gadkari *aji*. She hadn't really understood and shrugged helplessly. 'Doctor, can I make a call?' Jyoti asked.

'Sure'.

Jyoti dialed quickly and spoke urgently, though lucidly into the phone. At the other end Rashid sat back and mulled. His mind went back to another day when decisions had been made. When he had sought solace in those kind eyes. To think of the same eyes staring at death made him choke. '*Bhabhi*, we must trust the doctor. I feel we should let him proceed.'

Jyoti wiped away a tear as he hung up. She quickly assented to the procedure.

Dr. Patel hastened to add, 'You could get a little goofy after the procedure, you know confused.' He smiled and continued, 'I hope you aren't a rocket scientist.'

'No,' thought Anand Athavale. 'I came close to becoming a half-decent physician at one time!'

FATE again? But his father had a drinking problem. And that did harden the liver and triggered bloody vomit. So was it a natural course of events or FATE?

Why then, this GRIEF?

This ANXIETY?

Why not ACCEPTANCE?

Arjun's emotional override was in high gear. He actively recalled memories of his father, startled that they were fuzzy already.

He WANTED more time with his father. DESIRED it. COVETED it.

He had taken it for granted and wasn't ready to relinquish it.

Arjun grabbed his temples and squeezed, trying to make some sense of it all.

ANAND ATHAVALE

It was overcast and gloomy when Anand and Abhay set out for Dahanu. By the time the train had pulled into Dahanu station the tumescent clouds had exploded into cascading rain. Using magazines to shelter their heads from the rain which was decidedly angular in the stiff breeze; the two waited anxiously for the State Transport bus. They were on their way to the cottage hospital to make arrangements for the next six months. Their rural internship beginning in a week would be the culmination of their formal medical training. They would be qualified to ply their trade. That thought and the water trickling down his spine made Anand shiver slightly.

Finally the bus arrived. It had a rusty metal framed fish affixed to the front. The fish had a rather malevolent look; akin to the shark from "Jaws". Their co-passengers were predominantly tribals; Warlis that worked the fields and the *chikoo* orchards. The bus took off at a great speed, scattering all in its path. Despite the blinding rain, the driver took on the turns at high velocity, hugging the curb of the raised road. They reached the town center where the majority of the occupants alighted. The bus circled a huge *peepal* tree and veered right along the coast towards the cottage hospital.

Dahanu *taluka* was a verdant green oasis removed from the helter-skelter pace of Bombay. It had 49% of its land under forest cover evidenced by the dense monsoon soaked foliage around them. This ecologically sensitive area had a thriving agrarian economy. The landscape was dotted with *chikoo* and guava orchards. Coconut palms bent over in the hurried monsoon breeze. They reached the hospital; a modest fifty-bed edifice on the seashore. Landscaping had not been of immediate concern and weeds grew wild between the various buildings.

The watchman hurried them into Dr. Naik's cabin. Outpatient hours were on and they waited while the already slightly inebriated doctor finished up. The better-dressed patients were asked to come to his private rooms that evening for 'special care', which carried a 'special fee'. Dr. Naik walked them over to his bungalow.

'Listen,' he started, 'I don't need both of you here all the time. If one of you wants an extra week off that can be arranged. For fifty rupees I can arrange coverage.'

This appeared to be the price to look away and not notice the absence. Abhay, whose parents had recently departed for the Gulf, buying him an Enfield bike as an abandonment gift, promptly piped up stating that he planned to stay there all through. Anand stored the information away. The hospital had a straightforward layout. They would have a two-room bungalow as their quarters. It came with an ancient retainer, Gajri *bai*. She greeted them with toothy smiles and promptly informed them that she would be seeking a pay raise. Haggling with her brought a feeling of familiarity. Sensing that they had gotten a hang of the place, the boys took a picnic lunch to the beach as the sun tried to pierce the gray haze. They attempted a small swim but a few floating turds sent them scurrying to the shore. As evening approached they sought the chief medical officer to take his leave, promising to return in a week.

Their goodbyes were cut short as an ambulance careened into the compound. Orderlies rushed over to bring in a young man soaked in blood. Naik turned his head and saw brain matter staring back at him.

'*Isko idhar kaheko laaya. Chalo*, ambulance *tayar karo. Bambai bhejo*.'

He turned to the boys. 'Do me a favour. I will hang a saline drip and will you accompany this patient to Bombay? Take him to JJ. He has been hit by a bus; that one with a fish actually. No chance of surviving here.'

Before the yet to be blooded doctors could protest, they were all bundled into an ambulance and set out for Bombay. As if on cue the rain pelted down again. The ambulance made a short stop at the young man's hut and a crowd gathered to gape as an older woman, presumably the patient's mother wailed and beat her chest. Just as the doors were closing, she reached into the vehicle and pulled off a sheet, a gesture that revealed that the bleak prognosis was evident to all. Why waste a good sheet when the life was not going to be saved anyway.

The ambulance set off again. Prakash, the driver grumbled that this was his third trip to Mumbai and sahib had again bundled him off without any concern for his *chai-paani*. He alternated between this piteous litany and a vehement condemnation of the driving skills of the 'fish-bus' driver.

'Minister *ka sagewala hai. Madarchot ne itne accident kiye. Phir bhi saala, koi inquiry nahi. Suspension toh chhodo*,' he concluded with a shrug.

An hour into the journey Prakash stopped for tea; unmoved by the pleas of the terrified medicos. As they started again, the patient started gurgling; Abhay grabbed his handkerchief and mopped up some bloody liquid from the back of his throat. The patient's breathing got shallow as they entered Bombay. The bubbling blood in the patient's pharynx rendered mouth-to-mouth a non-option. They attempted to artificially ventilate the patient by elevating and depressing his arms. By the time they pulled into the casualty area of the JJ hospital the patient was cheyne-stoking. A horde of *mamas* descended on the ambulance and rushed the patient in. A tear-streaked Anand sat astride the patient, continuing his valiant efforts.

'Please save him, please save him', he mumbled.

A rather bored looking casualty medical officer sauntered in and looked at the patient from afar.

'Yeh toh mar gaya. Arre Tukya, morgue la kalav.'

Anand's eyes blazed, but the officer was gone; the mama had pulled out the IV. Abhay sat crestfallen in the corner. As they left the casualty area Abhay said, "I need a drink *yaar*".

Anand, an occasional partaker concurred. A brisk walk found them at Shetty's. After a few beers the day's proceedings faded, till they were only a tale to be told in the future.

The first month of their rural sojourn was stimulating. The sozzled CMO allowed them to do any and everything. The 'fish-bus' and the nearby train line kept them busy with trauma cases. Theoretical knowledge was easily being translated into technical skills and patient care. Abhay took the first shift 'on-call' till 1 am. Anand handled the less frequent later calls. They both got quite adept at handling snakebites, normal labor and minor surgery. An outbreak of dysentery and cholera honed their skills in fluid management. They even visited a nearby penitentiary to inoculate the inmates.

Anand began to feel that he could make a difference; that he could connect. The rush that comes from helping others became addictive. He put in extra hours at the hospital. He stridently pleaded with the tribal women to bring their afflicted young ones in soon, before the damage caused by dehydration was irreversible.

Anand often spent the early hours of the day on the beach. Watching the *koli* fishermen set out to set their nets had an innate rhythm; that set an upbeat tone for the day. As Abhay lolled, Anand strolled; dissipating restless energy and striving to add up to something. On the infrequent day that they both had the evening off they would clamber onto Abhay's bike and roam the shore, stopping at bars near the station to tank up before returning to the hospital. Nearby Gujarat was dry and daily commuters to Bombay often detrained at Dahanu for a quick tipple before resuming their journey home.

Anand took a weekend off and spent some time with his girlfriend Soma.

Soma was a couple years junior to him and they had connected while discussing the intricacies of Carnatic classical music. Soma Rast lived for the moment and Anand had established residence in a rather long one. She was indifferent to his obvious devotion, skirting any serious talk with her tinkling laughter and obtuse reference to an ex, Rajeev, whom she proclaimed had shown her true albeit temporary love. She also kept a separate existence with her 'cool crowd'; Anand was not part of that equation. The difference in social strata also did not help. Soma Rast was part of the with-it Napean Sea road crowd while Anand from Andheri was distinctly middle class.

"Andy from Andy' was the deprecating nickname the 'cool crowd' had for Soma's beau. But he plugged on.

This particular weekend found him animated as he discussed his experiences with Soma and her parents. They indulgently approved. The enthusiasm he felt for his profession was reassuring. When Anand returned, Abhay took a rare day off to visit an aunt. At two, a ward-boy knocked on the window of their bungalow, 'Call'. Anand changed and walked over to the female ward. He was directed to the labor room. Nurse Menon was on duty. She indicated that the patient on the table had been under Dr. Naik's 'special' care and had been in labor for 36 hours.

'The sun should not rise or set twice prior to delivery after a woman commences labor', Dr. Saraiya's accented tones floated through his brain.

A quick examination revealed a 'face presentation' and the patient was in obstructed labor. Anand sent a call over to Dr. Naik. The ward boy returned with the news that Dr. Naik was violently ill. Reading between the lines, Anand concluded that Dr. Naik was drunk beyond hope and asked nurse Menon to prepare the operation theatre. Sweating bullets, he performed a cesarean section, with nurse Gaekwad giving the ether anesthesia and nurse Menon, ably assisting/pointing the way. Anand cleaned up and walked over to the post-op bay. He noticed the fair skinned tribal for the first time. He rightly concluded that this was probably a result of the legendary 'out-reach' program at the Irani orchards, where octogenarian Parsi owner Boman Irani reached out for a tribal experience ever so often. A wizened old man sat next to the pale girl. The bonny, recently delivered baby, slept soundly besides his mother. The old man briskly got to his feet.

'I am Bhiku, her husband's father,' he said gesturing towards the sleeping girl. The old man suddenly dived for Anand's feet, 'Thank-you, thank you for saving her, and my grandchild. That drunken sod would have killed her. But the almighty sent you. I will name this grandchild Anand after you.'

Considerably embarrassed by this show of raw emotions, Anand helped the old man to his feet. A little girl sat next to him.

'This is Paro, my daughter's daughter. My daughter is sickly and I care for Paro. She is my *jaan*,' he said, fondly stroking her head. Paro sneaked a look around her grandfather's back and smiled cheekily.

Anand showed the old man the surgical incision. 'Keep this clean, don't let it get infected. In fact I want her,...'

'Bhingree' the old man volunteered,

'...to stay in the hospital for a few weeks, she lost a lot of blood and may need transfusions,' Anand concluded.

'I will give sir,' Bhiku proffered his arm streaked with veins bulging from a life of manual labour. Anand made arrangements for the transfusion. Bhiku would replace the blood used. A tired Anand retired, happy. The next few weeks both Anand and Abhay bonded with their new patient. Bhingree nursed her infant; they kept her wound scrupulously clean. However her baseline anemia rendered more profound by the recent blood loss was more refractory than expected.

When Anand pleaded with her husband to give blood the sullen man replied,

'Why don't you give her blood? You eat meat everyday, I survive on watery rice.'

Despite the fact that Anand and Abhay had both donated blood during the last month they gave blood again. Bhingree was transfused and her anemia improved. Her wound began to heal. Her husband came by repeatedly, trying to get the young fifteen-year-old mother discharged.

'I can't manage the farm and the house. My ailing sister is with us and Bhiku drinks away any money he can lay his hands on.'

Anand steadfastly refused, leaving standing instructions that he was to be called before Bhingree was discharged. Not quite cognizant of his rights the petulant young man gave in. Bhingree always looked relieved after these confrontations; she smiled her thanks and busied herself caring for her newborn, Anand.

Anand took another weekend off. After briefly visiting his family he set out for Gorai beach with Soma and her parents. Her father had the use of a company shack and Anand excitedly related the entire Bhingree story.

His fulfillment as a physician and a caregiver was readily apparent. Mrs. Hendricks presided over the shacks and rapidly dispatched one of her strapping lads to catch a ubiquitous piglet after Mr. Rast indicated that they would like *sorpatel* for dinner. The meal was satisfying; Anand had helped himself to a generous portion of Mr. Rast's imported scotch. The parents settled in for the night while the youngsters walked on the deserted moonlit beach. Soma lit a cigarette and passed it to Anand, who sociably pulled on it. They settled down on the beach; he put his hand around her and drew her close. Life was good. This was when she usually protested, but not this time. They hugged briefly. He held her close and kissed her, loving her beery breath. His lips found hers, again; she blew some of her inhaled smoke into his lungs. As he collapsed in a convulsion of coughs she ran into the ocean. Gathering himself, he pursued. He found her and drew her closer. The moon outlined her perky features; his hands cupped her breasts. She did not resist. Anand ventured further, but she pulled away. The magic of the moment passed. They walked back hand in hand to the shack. Soma disappeared inside; Anand curled up on the verandah. He looked up at the sky and sniffed the salty air. He could not remember when he had been happier. Sleep came easy, along with soporific dreams.

When Anand returned on Monday, Bhingree was gone. He scoured the grounds and ran through the wards, she was nowhere. Abhay confessed that he had skipped rounds on Sunday. The wards were light, the patients stable. Everything was on autopilot; Abhay had tended to emergencies diligently but otherwise had spent the day curled up in a hammock [another guilt gift from Dubai] with an interesting book. Anand was beside himself; he interrogated the nurses till they were in tears. Apparently Bhingree's husband had signed her out on Saturday; the nurse on duty saw the note to call him. But he was away, away in Gorai, away under the moon with Soma. He had let the husband take Bhingree. Anand excused himself from the bustling outpatient rooms. He talked to the ancillary staff, the Warlis gathered in the waiting room. Either there was no information or no one would talk.

Finally, Anand 'borrowed' Abhay's bike and rode off to the station. The 'fish-bus' almost got him but he veered off the road in time. He found a dark seat in the back of Swagat bar and courageously ordered a bottle of vodka. He diluted it with Fanta and sipped away. He liked the vodka; really liked it. This one was called Petrov; cost just fifty-five rupees. Did every vodka have to have a Russian name? This hooch was from Rae Bareilly. Anand was pretty sure that if he were to scour the streets of R. B. there was a pretty low probability of his bumping into a Petrov. He idly wondered, if Dagdu decided that his moonshine was vodka would he have to call it Dagduoff?

The owner of 'Swagat', a man with a large sickly family, plied him with snacks. Tandoori fish and boiled eggs. Anand looked at his glass somberly and grappled with his convulsing mind. He was sure she would perish. Her wound was still wet, it would get infected. Besides she was still anemic. That evening Abhay brought the ambulance around. Anand had passed out at the bar; the bottle of vodka was finished. For two weeks Anand would sneak away and drink during the day. He found a willing accomplice in Dr. Naik. They left the wards to Abhay and slipped out in one of the ambulances. They took to spending days in Silvasa, in Daman. Anand liked the vodka. It had a neutral taste and did not stink later.

Gajri *bai* promptly noted the change in Anand and with two fewer eyes watching her, she grew bolder in her larceny. At one meal Anand and Abhay just had fish heads and tails. Gajri *bai* had kept the prime pieces for herself.

Two weeks later Bhingree was back; her wound was infected and had dehisced. An apologetic Bhiku carried her in. Anand tearfully berated him, and rushed off to bathe the wound in peroxide. The next day he sent Abhay to Bombay for some stainless steel suture. He transfused her again, donating blood himself to replenish the depleted stock. He freshened the edges of the wound and heaped them together in an interrupted mattress suture. On the third day Bhingree's sister-in-law Chavi was brought in. She had third degree burns over half her body. Her husband had tired of her sickliness and had set her alight. Anand religiously dressed her wounds with a silver ointment and washed Bhingree's incision with peroxide till exuberant, pink, fresh granulation tissue was seen. Chavi was healing well too. Anand had contacted a philanthropic plastic surgeon in the city who had agreed to deal with her contractures.

One evening Chavi contracted a high fever. The call book the ward boy brought said, 'Patient breathless.'

Nurse Menon's codes were 'breathless' for a salvageable patient and 'gasping' for one that only needed to be pronounced. Anand rushed to the ward. Chavi was in septic shock. Paro gazed at her motionless mother with apprehensive eyes while Bhiku gnawed at his own interiors, watching his child suffer. At four, Chavi gave up her valiant struggle. The rampant septicemia claimed her. Bhiku allowed himself one outburst then he consoled his motherless grand-daughter who was now even more attached to his side. The loss of a care-giver and its importance was not lost on her, despite her tender years. Bhingree embraced her family. The cooing of the newborn Anand was like a balm for their gaping wounds.

In two weeks Bhingree was ready to be discharged. Anand had forgotten all about the liquor in the last few weeks. Bhingree's return to health was his personal triumph. Bhingree returned home. That weekend Bhiku came over to invite the doctors for a *satyanarayana puja*. He wanted to thank the creator for not taking it all away from him. Anand and Abhay went over on their bike. They were greeted warmly and shown to two plush throne-like chairs. A loudspeaker blared the latest Bollywood hit, testament to the merrymaking. Bhiku personally served the doctors. Paro ran around demanding hugs from the gathered well-wishers. Anand thought of the last time he had seen Soma. So much had happened since; he would go and see her the next weekend.

Two days later, Abhay had just returned from a normal delivery. It was 2 am, time for Anand to take over. The dreaded knock followed by the ward boy's dramatic, 'Call' jarred Anand awake. He walked over to the hospital. Bhiku was in the waiting room; Bhingree sat a little apart. Little Anand was suckling at her breast. Anand did not notice much initially. Bhiku held Paro; her face was turned away from him. That's when Anand noticed the blood. It was all over Bhiku. At Anand's urging Bhiku set Paro down. The jagged wound in her right thorax came into view. Pink lung bubbled in and out of it. Paro was frothing at the mouth. She flailed weakly on the table, settling down again after Bhiku gathered her up. His remorse filled, lined face was contorted with anguish. Anand rushed to organize an ambulance but Paro saved everybody the futility. She gasped once and ceased breathing comfortably in Bhiku's arms. Anand got the story from Bhingree a bit later. Bhiku had returned home from a bout of binge drinking. Only Paro was around. He begged her for more money. He raged and cajoled, wheedled and pleaded but she infuriated him by refusing to reveal Bhingree's secret stash. In his rage Bhiku swung an axe and struck the only reason he still lived. Bhiku stood before him, repugnant to himself. The police led the broken man away.

Two days later Anand disappeared again. Abhay found him wasted in a hotel room. That weekend he tried to get it together; to salvage the remnants of his psyche. He told Soma everything. She was horrified and commiserated but soon pleaded to be taken to the new Clint Eastwood movie. On the way there they talked about her new passion, 'The Hunger project'.

'It's a problem of distribution you know, not one of production', she informed him.

In the theatre she cuddled up cosily against his arm; Bhiku and Paro replaced by Hollywood glitz in her mind. Anand was unraveling. He felt disconnected and superfluous. He could not rationalize anything and was convinced that this was all his own, very own failure. Richard Burton bent down and Clint fired; a steely look in his eyes. Soma gasped. Anand's alienation was complete. He had stopped relating to his family for a while. Now it seemed that Soma and he inhabited different planets.

That night he returned to the hostel and ventured into Sonu and Amrut's room. Both wannabe psychiatrists dealt with current problems by philosophizing and smoking pot. After a few tokes, Sonu and Amrut felt that they had his dilemma cracked. Relatively sober, Anand was unconvinced.

He returned to Dahanu, unwilling but compelled. It was only a matter of time. One night a baby was stillborn. The father had noticed the smell on Anand's breath and pointed the finger. A police case was filed. Dr. Naik corroborated the facts and Anand was severely censured. He was summoned back to Bombay; he was not going to graduate. Soma refused to take his calls. He continued to drink and stopped calling her.

Two years later she won the Miss Asia title and sent Anand a newspaper clipping with a card which said, 'See what you missed.'

Anand threw it away. He didn't care anymore. Many years later he felt he saw her, gaping at him behind dark glasses from the back seat of her plush car. By then he was in the throes of his affair with the other Soma, 'Soma Ras'. In time, he secured a position with a pharmaceutical firm and became a well-compensated alcoholic. He functioned well during the day but needed a bit by the evening. His parents got him married; he never abused his wife or children. The only time he lost total control was when Naru died.

All of this crystallized in his mind as he was being wheeled into the angiography suite. Mrs. Athavale asked, 'What is this procedure called?' 'TIPSS' replied Dr. Patel, enunciating each letter individually. 'Transjugular intra-hepatic porto-systemic shunt.'

'Tips. Hanh. Nice name. TIPSS, a procedure for the tipsssy.' Anand Athavale thought wryly, his last coherent thought before the sedation-induced stupor took hold.

11

The jangle of the telephone intrusively interrupted the thick silence. Nakul looked up from his book and nodded; Arjun grabbed it.

'Hello! Yes. No... There are no nets today. All of us will be at the reception at the Indian ambassador's residence.'

Nakul looked at Arjun inquiringly. His eyebrows raised; he silently mouthed, 'Who is it?' Arjun gesticulated ignorance then continued, 'No, the team has not been decided Mr. Gupta. The playing eleven is announced just before the game by the captain.' There was a hiatus as Nakul darted up from the seat.

'How would I know? Why would you pay me? Once the team is announced everyone will know...'

The naïve youngster was taken aback as Nakul grabbed the phone and slammed it down. Nakul's voice conveyed consternation and anger.

'Don't talk to people you don't know.'

Arjun stammered not quite comprehending the situation, 'I thought... He said... he was a reporter, you know, one of the journalists.'

Nakul grabbed him urgently, 'Whatever! Don't talk to anyone then, particularly anything to do with the upcoming game.'

Enlightenment spread across Arjun's countenance. 'You mean he was one of those....Betting...... Fixing!'

Nakul held his hand up, signaling his final edict. 'I don't know and I don't want to find out.' Nakul gestured that the conversation was over and headed out.

The thought that anyone considered him even remotely venal, nauseated Arjun.

The entire team spent the day exploring Islamabad; a planned city carved out of the Margala hills. Barren and bleak institutional appearing bureaucratic buildings vied for space with Saudi financed mosques. The team paused outside the Faizal mosque, one of the largest in the Muslim world. Munaf's prattle was lost on Arjun; the convolutions in his personal life drew him further into their vortex.

The reception was held on the lawns of the embassy. The lights were bright and food was laid out on tables scattered across the lawn. Liveried waiters shuttled between conversing guests peddling soft drinks. There was a gentle flow of people to and fro across the carefully manicured lawns as the invitees mingled. The air was filled with tinkling laughter, the clink of glasses and mingling fragrances of the tittering women. The players were clustered at one end of the lawns, as dignitaries fawned over them and arranged themselves in various permutations and combinations for the busy shutterbugs. Arjun was singled out for more than customary attention. The invitees sensed the emergence of a new superstar. The popping flashlights blinded the young boy who temporarily forgot his personal agony and basked in the adulation.

The rather bulky man moved silently with an agility that belied his mass. Pausing to put an ear to the door, he appeared satisfied and let himself into the room easily. He gingerly stepped over and pulled the drapes shut. He surveyed the room and went to work. Knowing exactly what he was looking for, he opened and shut drawers taking care to carefully replace any articles he disturbed. He meticulously examined each dresser and then moved over to the suitcases. Fifteen minutes passed. The man glanced at his wristwatch. The dial glowed in the dark and he didn't like what he saw. He resumed his search with renewed urgency. Rummaging through a cluttered kitbag he was now not as intent in keeping order. He was confident that the mess in front of him defied any method and let out a low whistle as he hit pay dirt. He reached in and quickly transferred something into a plastic shopping bag he had produced from a pocket with a flick of his wrist. Then allowing himself a "phew" as the gamey scent from the kitbag assailed him, he stood up and surveyed the room to make sure everything was in order. He left as quietly as he had entered; he had been in the room for exactly twenty-two minutes.

The initial pops escaped everyone's attention; the gaiety of the gala was infectious. The smiles were broader, the bonhomie palpable. The second series were louder bangs and sounded closer. A no-nonsense security squad quickly surrounded the Indian team. They politely, but rapidly ushered the players to the rear of the building and stuffed them into limousines that appeared to have been waiting. Then, surrounded by paramilitary jeeps filled with men that scanned the environs with cold steely looks; the limousines silently melted into the night.

Taking a circuitous route they reached the service entrance of the hotel. Again the security squad deployed with liquid precision; forming a protective curtain around the perplexed and slightly scared cricketers. They entered the lobby through the rear and made for the bank of elevators to the right. The entourage waited for a rather large man with a shopping bag, flanked by two tartly made-up women to pass.

Arjun gasped and nudged Nakul. 'Those women, they are from the coffee shop in Karachi.'

Nakul looked at them and nodded assent. They were the same women!

The security squad escorted the players to their rooms and assumed positions in the hallways. The players soon settled in wondering what the disturbance outside the embassy had been. The final game was two days later, a day-night affair in Lahore. The series had been peaceful, the crowds exemplary. It would be a shame if it ended on a sour note.

The skipper was glad that the party had terminated early; his boys could do with the rest. He gave his mind to planning the final match. If he won the toss…. He drifted away.

Arjun sank down on his bed. He had changed and wondered if he should call the hospital to find out how his father was doing. Nakul was curled up in bed.

He mumbled, 'If you are planning to call, do it soon. We should get a good night's sleep.'

Arjun's eye was fixated on his kitbag. Something wasn't kosher. He muttered, 'Suchen is back, I probably won't be playing the next game.'

What followed can only be described as a cross between a shriek and a scream.

Nakul bolted upright, 'Surely it's not the end of…' He looked at Arjun rummaging through his kitbag.

'They're gone, they are fucking gone.'

'What… and language please!' Nakul attempted to bring some sanity to the proceedings.

There was a low but urgent knock on the door. 'Everything all right sir?'

Nakul sprang up and opened the door. 'Yes' he said as the strapping guard pushed him aside and peered into the room.

'The youngster, very excitable,' Nakul offered by way of explanation.

Seemingly satisfied the guard stepped out.

'My gloves, they are gone. Someone stole them. I had checked before I left and they were there. And the zipper was open when we got back.'

The jangling telephone interrupted the tearful boy. It was Arjun's mother to tell him that his father had tolerated the procedure well and was recovering.

'The doctors say he is stable,' she concluded.

The anguish of a moment ago vanished as the boy beamed with the good news. The next few minutes were spent rejoicing in the glad tidings. Arjun only remembered his missing gloves when Pranay was on the line sharing his excruciatingly detailed insightful pearls of wisdom with his buddy. He was still trying to communicate some last minute advice when Arjun quickly updated Pranay with the latest happenings. While discussing the truant gloves and the fact that only a few knew or could guess that they were more than mere gloves; they both had a coincident intuitive burst of inspiration.

'Rahim!' they exclaimed in unison.

'Who else,' argued Pranay?

'I don't know. How could Rahim know?' Arjun could not comprehend how.

'Let me investigate a bit, I'll call back. Don't leave your room,' Pranay instructed.

'OK,' Arjun promised.

As he put the phone down in its cradle, Nakul sat before him demanding an explanation. Arjun was long winded and Nakul incredulous.

'You mean, you think you can bat well only because of the gloves.'

Arjun nodded emphatically, 'I don't think, I know. I was nobody till I got the gloves. Really...,' he pleaded with Nakul to believe him. Nakul tut-

tutted but seeing that the young lad was resolute in his conviction, he in turn suggested.

'Well, we have an easy fix then. We will just ask Suchen to give you another pair.'

'No,' groaned Arjun, 'That will not be the same. Not all gloves are magical.'

Nakul looked at him disbelievingly, 'MAGICAL, are you for real? I.. you are being difficult. What are you doing now?'

Arjun had crept to the door and had opened it a crack. He put an eye to the fissure and scanned the hallway.

'I must find them. I have to get out.' Arjun sounded desperate; the hallway was crawling with over zealous security personnel.

'But where will you start looking.' Nakul posed the proverbial million dollar question.

12

The next morning, a plan was shaping up. Pranay knew where to begin, but hesitated to venture out by himself. He ran over to Pallavi and tried to explain the situation. Pallavi's excitement level was directly reflected in her voice and her every startled 'What?' increased in pitch and volume.

Nervously shushing her, Pranay ushered her out. 'What should we do?'

Pallavi did not hesitate for a moment. 'We must confront Rahim. *Saala izzat ka saval hai.*'

'Alright then, but drop the *tapori bambaiya Hindi.*' Pallavi shrugged and they walked away together without any further ado.

They found Rahim lounging around at the street corner. He had a burnt matchstick clenched between his teeth, a scarf tied rakishly around his neck. He struck a macho pose and asked,

'*Arre sun Pranay. Woh Arjun ka baap. Tabiyat theek toh hain na?*'

Pallavi pushed Pranay aside and tried to stand chin to chin with the towering Rahim. 'No thanks to you,' she retorted.

'*Matlab?*' said a confused Rahim.

'*Acha, saala* innocent *banne ka* try *mat karo.* I know *kitne paani mein...* I mean how much water you are in.' Pallavi's convent-learnt Hindi let her down.

'*Kya bakwas kar rahi hain,*' the incredulous Rahim now turned to Pranay.

'Don't kid around. What have you done with the gloves?' Pranay attempted a tough veneer.

'*Arre kuch barabar baat kar*, tell me what happened.' Rahim finally dropped the swaggery tough talk.

Now quite adept at this, Pranay obliged and finished with, 'Now tell me, who else could be responsible for this? Who else would know?'

Rahim started out outraged, '*Arre saala, mein idhar woh udhar*. What did you think I am superman or what? Just because I am Muslim.'

'You guys always support Pakistan,' Pallavi blurted.

Then seeing the enraged Rahim she bit her tongue.

'*Bas bahut hua! Saala mussalman hoon to maine he kiya hoga*,' Rahim roared, '*Main to purani dushmani chodke Arjun aur India ko* cheer *kar raha tha*. Isn't it amazing that despite everything we do to assimilate, at the first hint of wrong doing, it is our fault. *Saala, musibat mein mera baap hi madat karta hain, phir bhi….. Uska kya?*'

Pallavi looked contrite and close to tears. Just then Pakya stepped out from behind the shadows of the tea stall. His countenance betrayed his feelings. In a small voice he said,

'I think it was my fault. Just yesterday I was at Bandu Gawli's *adda* and placed a bet on India winning the final match.'

Rahim wasn't in a mood to listen, '*Saala, maine bhi paisa daala*. Now tell me would I sabotage that. Doubt my nationalism, *lekin jab paise ka sawal hain.*'

'Let me hear what Pakya has to say,' Pranay thundered.

'Bandu Gawli was amazed at the size of my wager.'

'Yah, Bandu said, '*Bahut* confidence *se paisa dal rahe ho bachche*'..

So I told him, '*Jab tak woh* gloves *hain, Arjun maarte rahega.*'

'He demanded an explanation. I … I .. I told him how well Arjun batted with the smelly gloves and how he could not reproduce that form without them. Yes, you see, I watched you both, your little experiment behind the building, before Rahim arrived. That's why I picked up the gloves from the *raddiwala*. But they did not work for me.'

'Bandu Gawli!' Pranay interrupted the sorry soliloquy. Rahim looked a bit flustered and attempted a peeved and hurt look.

'Bandu Gawli! Come Pallavi.' Pranay turned away.

'Wait, I'll come too, I know Bandu Gawli,' an enthused Rahim followed.

'Can I help,' Pakya volunteered'.

Pallavi bestowed on him her best icy look. 'I think you have done enough!'

The kids charged off leaving a woebegone Pakya in their wake. Bandu Gawli's gambling den was a small shelter behind a broken down wall. A torn bedspread was propped by two bamboos of unequal length to provide some protection from the sun. Under this lay sprawled on a charpoy, his general demeanor befitting royalty, Bandu Gawli. A minion with a suitably scared look scurried around. He carried a dog-eared book probably for recording bets. Gawli was bare-chested and had a *lungi* wrapped around his waist. When the kids reached there he was engaged in watching his enormous biceps flex. First left, then right, pausing only momentarily to dislodge an irritating bugger and chase away a persistent fly. His eyes lit up when he saw Rahim.

'*Arre bachche, Kya kamaal ki news laya woh Pakya.* Did you send him?'

Rahim was quick to deny this, casting a wary look at the glowering Pallavi.

Bandu continued, 'Gupta *saab* was delighted. Oddly he has raised the stakes against India winning despite the news about the gloves. He said don't worry and has promised me a five thousand rupee gift. Just for keeping my ear to the ground.'

'Gupta,' mumbled Rahim, for lack of anything better to say.

'*Haan Gupta, Bada jadiya aadmi hain.* But he is tough.'

'Where can we meet him?' Pranay asked tentatively.

'*Woh idhar kahan?*' Bandu sat up, relishing the fact that he had an attentive audience. '*Woh to udhar hain.* You know the other day, when that young Indian player was photographed with those women. Those are his girls. He tries to get close to the players through them too. Anyway why do you want to know all this? Rahim, why don't you introduce me to your friends? *Arre*, you two want to bet some money? I will give you good odds. Gupta is sure India will lose the last game.'

Pranay hurriedly walked away shepherding the inquisitive Pallavi, who wanted to find out how the odds were calculated.

Rahim waved halfheartedly to Bandu, '*Chalta hoon bhai,*' he said in farewell, but Bandu had already settled back into his flexing routine. The minion scuttled off to organize some tea and Rahim hurried after the other kids.

Rahim reached home and his brain sizzled. Why was he never accepted? It was good riddance to that Athavale kid anyway. Sentimental value, he had said about the gloves. He wanted to feel good but the lump at the bottom of his stomach would not budge. Finally he gave up and dialed his father in Pakistan.

Darkness was already on them as Arjun and Nakul returned to their room after evening nets. Nakul got some icepacks for his knees while Arjun peered out of the window. He had just gotten off the phone with an excited Pranay and a perennially interrupting Pallavi. He finally could piece the story together; Gupta had taken his gloves.

As he hung up and brought Nakul up to date, he abruptly jumped up. 'Of course it was Gupta. Remember we saw those two women in the lobby. Maybe the fat guy with them was Gupta.'

Nakul nodded, it did make sense. 'What next. Why don't you forget about the gloves? Surely you are not that superstitious,' he begged.

Now charged, his eyes glistened wildly Arjun said, "Gupta followed me to Islamabad from Karachi. I am sure he will be there in Lahore. I am going to devise a way of getting my gloves back.'

Nakul thankfully settled in, rightfully thinking that there would be no more action that night. Arjun tossed and turned and was still awake when the early dawn insinuated itself between the drapes.

The next day was a whirlwind of activity. The team took a short flight to Lahore, the capital of Pakistani Punjab. Just a few kilometers from the India border it was the cultural and artistic capital of the nation. On the ride from the airport to the hotel a pleasing medley of Islamic and British architecture flashed by. Munaf was quick to point out the Badshahi mosque, Shalimar gardens, Lahore fort and Emperor Jehangir's tomb.

Arjun had a pleasant surprise at the hotel. Rashid *chacha's* smiling, familiar face. He exchanged a few words. Rashid *chacha* had news. He had made some inquiries. Arjun listened excitedly but soon skipper beckoned. His creased brow betrayed his concern. He wanted his boys to rest. Arjun hurried over to him.

After settling into their rooms, the captain called for nets and a team meeting, which went through dinner. Nakul had hoped Arjun had forgotten about the gloves. Apparently not. When they returned to their room, Arjun sat down for a brief moment. He then bounded up. He checked the hallway outside their room; it was crawling with security personnel again. Irfan and Imran were there too, laconic exteriors in place. The others sauntered about idly chatting. Some sipped tea; a long night's vigil lay ahead. Explaining his need to go out at this late hour and asking to be allowed to do so alone, appeared to be impossible. He stepped back into the hotel room and sank down on his bed dejected.

'What now?' Nakul echoed Arjun's thoughts.

Arjun looked despondent. He looked up and his eyes strayed to the small balcony attached to the room. Nakul followed his eyes and sat up with a startled, 'No!' as Arjun's next move became apparent.

Arjun had already bounded up and stepped out onto the balcony. He peered down from the third floor. There was nothing to break his fall; a few broken bones were assured if he just jumped. A car pulled up and three men alighted. The driver of the car joined them after a moment. The four men were engaged in earnest conversation under the awning. Arjun looked to the other side, a drainpipe led straight down. His thoughts strayed back to another tempestuous night; where the gloves and a drainpipe were also involved. All that seemed eons ago.

Without another thought he climbed over the railing and holding onto it, reached over to the drainpipe.

'Are you mad?' Nakul had followed him out onto the balcony and now whispered urgently. Arjun smiled back and grabbed the drainpipe decisively. He began to descend carefully. Nakul looked over the railing.

'Alright, I am coming too.' The stage whisper again.

'Wait for me near the hedge on the other side of the road.' Nakul decided to take charge. 'Don't let anybody see you.'

'I have to look for Munaf,' Arjun whispered back as he slithered down the pipe, momentarily losing balance. He landed on the soft ground with a gentle thud and took a moment to gather himself. Then he darted across the drive and crouched next to a dense shrub. Nakul followed him. His descent was more deliberate; a bit like his batting. He stepped down, brushed himself and started walking across the drive. He had been so preoccupied with his deadly drop that he had failed to notice the little meeting under the canopy breaking up. Two men had stepped into the hotel. The driver and his companion jauntily returned to the running automobile. He let himself in and opened the passenger seat for his companion. The doors slammed shut, eerily loud; the car revved and proceeded down the driveway. He braked suddenly as Arjun confidently stepped out of the shadows, just as he rounded the corner of the drive. He stopped the car and stepped out indignantly.

'What the...' he began, his features softened as he recognized the Indian star. 'Well, what have we here! The child prodigy trying to sneak a night out on town. Can I give you a ride somewhere?'

'Hello Azam,' Arjun mumbled to the Pakistani captain.

'What brings you here at this late hour?' Azam chuckled, 'Forget about me. I am a local lad just meeting up with some well-wishers. So, do you want that ride or is this some top secret rendezvous?' The passenger side door opened and a familiar voice said, 'Beta it's OK. We will drive you. '

Rashid *chacha*!

Arjun looked up decisively. 'As a matter of fact we do need a ride.' He gestured to the hitherto hidden Nakul to join him. As Nakul stepped into the light, Azam let out another low whistle.

'Mr. Clean too. This just keeps getting more and more intriguing. *Rashid bhai aap toh kuch batate bhi nahin,*' Nakul gestured towards the car.

'Arjun has forgotten something. We need to retrieve it,' he volunteered by way of an explanation. He got into the back seat next to Arjun.

'*Abhi chalo bhi Azam mian,*' Rashid cajoled.

'Wait Azam *bhai,*' a voice urged. Munaf came running down the drive and nodded to Arjun. He stopped short, perplexed at seeing Nakul and Arjun getting into Azam's Lexus.

'What do you want?' an irritated Azam questioned.

'Just a lift to my hotel, if it is on your way back from wherever you are taking my friends, if it is not too much bother, if...'

'Just get in,' Azam commanded and Munaf scurried in next to Arjun. Arjun gave him a knowing smile and looked away.

Munaf whispered to him, 'I have been waiting. You know what you asked me at dinner! I spoke to your friend Rashid *bhai.* He has done some business with Gupta before and he told me where Gupta may be. I think he is right. I have seen those two women in Diamond bazaar.'

Two blocks later Rashid got out and Nakul went in the front. Rashid leaned through the open window and whispered into Arjun's ear. 'Best of luck. I wish I could accompany. But....I may be watched and it is best that we part ways here. Azam thinks this is some kind of dare, which you have been challenged to accomplish by the team!'

Rashid looked long at the diminishing tail-lights. The boy had his father's kind eyes.

Diamond bazaar, is a red light district known for its dancing girls. In Pakistan, prostitution was not only illegal, it was rampant too. It took more than a few laws to rein in the oldest profession. After Nakul told Azam of their destination, Azam allowed himself another low whistle. Then silence reigned for a while in the plush interior of the car. It was only interrupted by Azam's sly persistent questions and Nakul's monosyllabic answers. Arjun gazed resolutely out the window. Munaf knew no details but was now sure he was part of some deep diabolical event and fervently hoped that his information was correct.

The car screeched to a halt outside a garish building. Some of the surrounding establishments were still open for business. Muted music and the jingle of dancing nautch girls defied soundproof walls and added to the somber mood. Street side vendors deftly folded betel leaves and handed them to customers who flitted about with averted faces. Nakul and Arjun stepped out unsure about how to proceed. The establishment identified by Munaf was cloaked in darkness. A solitary window on the upper floor emitted a weak yellow glow through a dusty window. The light went off just as they looked up.

'Do you want me to wait,' asked Azam. His eyes were twinkling at the duo's discomfort.

'If you don't mind, we may need the ride back. Why don't you park around the corner somewhere? We will find you.' Nakul replied tersely.

Arjun turned around to talk to him. Just then the front door of the building opened and a large figure flanked by two women walked towards a swank Benz. Gupta and his molls. With much tittering they got in and sped off.

'Pull up around the corner and wait, give us ten minutes.' Nakul whispered to Azam and turned away.

Azam looked at him wryly, 'Nothing illegal I hope, *bhai*.' Nakul looked back and met his inquisitive gaze with steely eyes before turning away.

Arjun followed and they scampered up a few steps and gingerly tried the door. It was locked, the door refused to budge.

Nakul stepped back a moment, 'We will have to try the window. You are smaller; here let me give you a leg up.' Nakul stopped beneath the window and cupped his hands, motioning for Arjun to step on them. Arjun did so gingerly and grunting, Nakul heaved as Arjun's fingers clawed at the windowsill for a hold. With a final grunt Nakul pushed, grimacing. Arjun pulled himself onto the sill as Nakul fell back. The window was open and Arjun was in, in a trice. The light flickered on for what seemed an eternity before it went off abruptly as Arjun stepped back out of the window triumphantly waving the grimy gloves. He stuffed them down his shirtfront and jumped down just as Azam and Munaf turned the corner.

'What's keeping you? We have a game tomorrow in case it slipped your mind. I want you both to get a good night's sleep; so you won't have any excuse when we whup your behinds.'

Nakul gestured to Azam to stop. 'No one is in. Too late. We will have to come back tomorrow. Well too bad, let's go.'

He walked by a dazed Azam and an open mouthed Munaf. A giggling Arjun followed. After dropping Munaf, the car deposited the duo outside the hotel. Thanking Azam profusely, the two skipped in and urgently summoned an elevator. Azam drove off shaking his head, a smile on his ample face as he contemplated the evening's goings-on. Nakul and Arjun stepped off the elevator and walked past a flabbergasted security detail, smiling cheerily and disappearing into their room with merry 'Good nights'. Nakul was all business, 'Now enough is enough, off to bed. Thank god tomorrow is a day night fixture'.

13

Rabi Mantri welcomed the TV audience for the final one dayer. 'Welcome to Lahore for the final one day international. It has been a terrific series so far and the final game promises to be just as interesting. The Indian side faced a selection dilemma with the return of Suchen. However it has resolved by itself. Jugraj Singh injured his left hand during fielding practice and will not play, making way for Suchen. We do have a bit of good news. Arjun's father underwent a life saving procedure yesterday and he is in stable condition. The Pakistan side is unchanged.'

The stands were filled with politicians and film stars from India who had hopped across the border for the game. They alternated between hiding behind over-sized designer sunglasses and waving to the adoring crowds. The lush green outfield looked like a layer of finely chopped mint chutney spread across an oval *paratha*. The pulsating crowd was impatient. A smell of roasted peanuts permeated the air. Clouds were suspended above the field like bubbles arising from the rinsing sunlight. A tied series, goodwill oozing out of every pore, an air of expectancy; the atmosphere was charged. Even the *gulmohurs* danced excitedly in the wind, shouting bawdy encouragement.

The game began. Pakistan batted first. Nasir Ahmed their opener finally found his stride. The Indian bowling held no demons for him. He scored with impunity on both sides of the wicket and in the latter stages of their innings he was ably aided by some lusty hitting by his skipper Azam. Pakistan amassed a gargantuan 312 in the allotted 50 overs.

'Slept well?' Azam queried, nudging Arjun as he walked back with the

Indian fielders.

Arjun gasped and looked away. Nakul gave him a stony stare.

Sujay Wandrekar summed up the afternoon's proceedings. 'A masterful display of one day batting from an under-rated Pakistani side. India may have let this one get away. Their behemoth of a batting line up will have to click in unison. To add insult to injury, Suchen has re-injured his thumb while fielding. It has been splinted and he could bat if required; probably lower down in the batting order.'

As the players had a light dinner the floodlights came on for the night session. The Indian opening pair walked out to bat and was sportingly cheered by a home crowd that had scented victory. The first two fiery overs from the super speedster Shohail Akbar saw the exit of the Indian openers. The crowd was on its feet.

Nakul and Arjun steadied the innings. Every ball bowled, particularly by Akbar was greeted with a crescendo of claps that culminated in a collective 'Ooh' as ball after ball whizzed by the Indian pair's ears. While Nakul batted with panache, Arjun was having a lot of difficulty with his gloves. They were torn in numerous places and appeared precariously close to falling apart. As the slower Wazir Khan replaced Akbar, bits of the gloves kept falling off in his first over causing stoppages in play. The umpire asked Nakul at the non-strikers end whether Arjun would like a new pair. The batsmen conferred in the middle of the wicket.

'Enough already? Get rid of those gloves. If you want, I'll ask Suchen to give you another pair.'

'NO!' Arjun pleaded, 'I mean it's got to be these gloves. They are lucky.'

Nakul looked at the gloves. 'You are going to get injured; besides there's not much of them left.'

Arjun hastily walked away, 'I am all right. Really...'

The game resumed. Arjun kept his tattered gloves on, ignoring the inquisitive stares of the Pakistani fielders. India reached 150 in 25 overs. Nakul got to his 100 with a beautifully timed cover drive. Acknowledging the crowd's applause, he waved his bat to the rest of his applauding teammates. Shohail came back with a beauty of a slower yorker and the dismayed Nakul watched his off stump do a slow-mo cartwheel to the keeper. Shohail jumped with joy and vigorously pointed the way back to the clubhouse. Nakul walked back dejectedly. The pumped up Shohail had more tricks up his sleeve. He reduced the Indian side to 212 for 8 in 40 overs with Arjun resolutely holding his ground.

The injured Suchen joined Arjun. As Arjun walked out to talk to his idol, his right glove finally threw in the towel. It disintegrated into fragments and the entire glove fell off his hand. The distraught youngster was in tears. Suchen put a comforting hand on Arjun's shoulder.

'What's the matter? You can change your gloves.'

The words tumbled out of Arjun fast and furious punctuated by wracking sobs. 'You don't understand. These are your gloves. You threw them away. I have only been batting well because of them.'

Suchen asked him to slow down and the elegiac Arjun quickly explained the saga of the gloves again. '....and last night we went to that Gupta's *adda* and got them.'

One of the Pakistani players was changing his shoes and others had grabbed the moment to partake of a few refreshing drinks. The two batsmen stood huddled as Arjun concluded.

Suchen laughed out loud, 'You really believe that. I can easily fix that. I'll give you another pair.' He gestured to the pavilion and turned back to Arjun.

'You know, that is humbug. You are good. All these strokes, this talent; its all you. This is your *karmabhoomi*. I firmly believe that all of us have been sent to earth for a purpose. Feel within yourself and know it. Remember, all one can do is to perform one's prescribed duty. Become self-realized. The only reward you need is fulfilling your potential. Everything else is incidental. As always there will be ups and downs, you will have good and bad times both on and off the field. But what you must believe in is yourself.'

Suchen paused as one of the reserves ran onto the field with a pair of gloves. Suchen took them from him and handed them to Arjun.

'Here, another one of my favorite pair, all yours.'

In the commentary box the long stoppage was causing consternation. 'A long pow wow between the world's greatest batsman and one of the most promising newcomers. Rather a long stoppage. They should have probably taken drinks. Wonder what that was all about. Probably strategy for the last 10 overs,' Mantri postulated.

'The simplest strategy would be to not get out. Of course they need the runs,' added Wandrekar.

The game resumed. Arjun pulled on his new gloves and settled into his stance. His mind was not in the game, Suchen's words whirled around in his mind, interspersed with montages of the monks at Taxila, his mother's face at Naru's funeral, his father's defeated eyes when he couldn't hold himself upright in the evening. He looked up to see the next ball upon him. 'CHIK'; a loud snick wobbled over to Nasir at gully. Nasir celebrated before seeing the ball straight into his hands. The ball bounced out and Arjun exulted in his reprieve. His brain would not settle, the mental flagellations continued. He just had the last ball to face.

His life accelerated in grainy frames through his confused brain.

'Chik,' another snick. This one fast and low to Nasir's right.

Nasir was determined to make amends. His concentration collided with the spurt of adrenaline that shot into his system. He overcompensated and his cupped hands closed over before the white orb reached them. As the ball trickled away from him, Nasir looked woebegone. His batting heroics were a distant memory. At the end of the over, Arjun's mind cleared like an amazing chemistry experiment.

Everything was suddenly clear. There was nothing he could do about the hand he was dealt. But the way he played it, would characterize the course of his life. His mind swung back to summer afternoons when the family settled down on the cool granite floor under a whirring fan and played bridge while sucking on mangoes. The discussions at the end of every deal; the post mortem of the game always revolved around 'what ifs' and 'you should have'. The perpetually and irritatingly right Pallavi would wax eloquent.

Arjun's father always maintained, 'Maybe that was how YOU had to play this deal. Now you have learn't from it. With this experience you will continually modify your game, constantly improving. It will always be your game and your way of playing it. You can't help but get better if you allow yourself to learn.'

It was his life and he and only he could direct it. He could not control the uncontrollable. But the rest, he would.

It was his duty to use his ABILITY, his TALENT. FATE and DESTINY, [if they really existed], were out of his control.

His Potemkin world crumbled around him; crumbled and grew new dimensions, a third, a fourth.

Like Abhimanyu, he would take care of the HERE and NOW and leave the rest to providence. The transiency of his TIME rapidly came into focus as happy memories of Naru barged in. Beautiful, surreal memories. People, places and times. His TIME was now. His GOOD FORTUNE had to be cashed in today. No time for WHAT IFS. He was at the crest of the RIDE. He had to ride the momentum, harness the energy.

Yes, there were MAYBES and GRAYS. He was tired of binary thinking. He embraced them. They were COMPROMISES and CHOICES that armed him for self determination.

MEMORIES again. Compromises his mother had made that were abundantly clear to all thanks to Savitri kaki's snide asides about blind men. Choices his father had made as he fell prey to an addiction that was now his only solace. Time, which had taken his brother from him.

If FATE wanted to have her way, it would be after he had a chance to have his say, after his own individual effort.

The pieces of the puzzle whirled furiously then slowed and settled into a coherent, meaningful pattern.

To WANT, To DESIRE, To COVET. He would channel these into positive attributes.

His anachronistic thoughts flipped and cartwheeled. An order was established.

He WANTED it now! Was he some unwitting conduit for something great? What if he was not. Would any of this change anything, bring his brother back, erase the lines from his mother's face, soften his father's hard liver? Probably not. Definitely not. Then why? Because. Such is the randomness of the word that in seeking a path to follow he had not seen his own path. HE WANTED IT!

For Naru, for Aai, for Baba..........for himself!

The puzzle was finished. The final piece fit. The picture was complete.

Arjun signaled for a reserve, who ran out and listened to his vital words. The reserve ran back and disappeared into the dressing room. He spoke to Nakul with some urgency. Nakul comprehended immediately. He walked over and rummaged through Arjun's bag, finally handing over a packet to him. Suchen got 16 from the over with four 4s. He winced with every stroke. The reverberations through his arm caused significant discomfort.

At the end of the over, the by now breathless reserve ran back onto the field and handed Arjun the packet. Arjun took his father's gift out and waved it. The television cameras followed his movements and the sight of the gloves brought a smile to his ailing father's face as he recuperated in his hospital bed, his family gathered with him to watch the game. Suchen walked over, 'So I am not lucky anymore?'

Arjun gazed directly into his eyes. The youngster's confidence and maturity impressed the veteran.

'I now know my karma. I must be the one who shapes it. I can and will define it,' Arjun asserted resolutely, as he wore his new gloves.

The game resumed, the tension mounted. Suddenly Arjun was strokeless and looked very uncomfortable in the middle. He was hit often; bleeding from a cut on the face, the result of a rearing snorter from Shohail. The blood slowly oozing out of the split skin on his cheekbone sucked him inwards. His concentration reached its zenith. He felt each drop of blood well up and ooze out onto the precipice of his gash, hanging precariously for a moment before succumbing to the lure of gravity; he felt as though he was in a trance. Suchen continued to score. Arjun looked unwavering, he was battered and bruised. With every blow that his adolescent body took, he gained strength. The Pakistani fielders smelt blood; literally. Their sledging was ruthless. They even verbalized invidious comparisons to a polio-stricken strokeless number eleven of yester years. They sensed that all that stood between them and victory was not Suchen, but Arjun.

In the last eight overs Arjun took more hits to his body than to his bat. His bearing was now that of a resolute boxer. Mrs. Athavale had her head burrowed in her sari. She couldn't bear to watch the carnage.

Pranay was proud, 'That is what he is all about,' he beamed to anyone who cared to listen.

Eight runs were needed off the last over to win. The Indian team sensed a historic victory and lined the balcony of their dressing room. A few were gnawing on the remnants of their nails; others were done with the nails and had started on the hardened skin around them. Suchen got 4 of the first ball. Shakir held the next one back. Suchen mistimed it and skied it to mid off, the fielder just made the catch jubilantly as the batsmen crossed over.

The last man walked to the non-striker's end. Shakir dug the next one in and Arjun took it on his ribcage doubling over in pain. His eyes glassed over. He remembered nothing. Not his castigating father, his unconditionally loving mother, Pranay's advice or Pallavi's prophecies. There was a steely calm in Arjun's brain as he limped away from the crease and tried to regain some external composure.

Shakir trundled in, shirt billowing in the wind and delivered a beautiful yorker with the next. Arjun lunged forward and took it on his shoe. A loud appeal was turned down; replays showed that the ball may have just missed the leg stump. Shakir walked back thoughtfully and dug the next one in short again. The ball flew off a bit of rough and thudded onto Arjun's helmet. Arjun crashed to the ground. His mother screamed. He lay there unseeing, unknowing. He no longer felt like an interloper. This was his moment; he just knew it.

The Indian trainer and the Pakistani team physician rushed onto the field. Arjun stood up looking decidedly concussed and wobbly. There was just one ball left. He waved the beseeching trainer back to the clubhouse. Abruptly his mind went back to Mohenjo daro, to Taxila. Like an old television set warming up, his thoughts clarified in incremental spurts. He understood the arrogance of the enlightened one. There was no one correct path. He had to choose his own. By making it his own, it became *his* correct path. That was the only reality. That and the finality of death were the only certainties, only realities. His insignificance was still of little doubt; but he felt in charge of his destiny. He felt alive. His whole being was focused at one spot that was his epicenter. His thoughts were no longer ephemeral. They crystallized into truth pebbles that seemed to be concentrated in the midst of his body. He could feel them in his chest, like hard to swallow food. He was submerged in them. Not suffocated but refreshingly immersed.

As he comported himself into his stance, his bearing was sangfroid. The excited crowd settled down and there was a hush as Shakir walked back to the top of his run up. This one was a beautiful outswinger. Arjun saw it framed in a halo of bright light. The ball was large and multicolored. As it bounced towards him he felt that he could see the world furiously spinning in it. He saw his life in accelerated slow motion. His own strengths and weaknesses were distinctly defined. Thoughts about himself quickly segued into others. His father's life an open book. His mother's sacrifices even more evident. His love for Pallavi, Pranay, Rahim, why even Pakya glaringly obvious. Hope and despair walked side by side like fraternal twins. He lunged forward. His pad wobbled and a large drop of sweat flew off his face.

The click of the snick overrode the ambient cacophony as the ball flew off the edge. The game proceeded in slow motion. He turned to watch the ball. The seam rolled hypnotically. The images in his brain whirred and turned along with him. They kaliedoscoped and settled. The ball glanced off the tippy tips of the lunging hapless Nasir and sped towards third man. Arjun charged down the pitch as the ball careened towards the ropes. A sprinting Shohail raced around the arc and was airborne in a desperate dive. The ball took an awkward bounce and the desperate Shohail flailed at it. Outstretched hand extended towards speeding orb. The hoardings lining the boundary seemed to converge on the ball. The small speck was indistinct in the melee as Arjun grounded his bat and turned around for a second run. The sunlight, the noises, the faces, the past, the present and the future all came together in a shining incandescent glow and he felt no more. Saw no more. Pandemonium erupted as the crowds emptied onto the field.

The hospital room was bright and airy. Sunlight poured in through the open window. Mr. Athavale's medicines were laid out in a neat row on his bedside table. Outside his open window a nasal vendor urged housewives to buy fresh bananas. Arjun rushed in, breathless,

'*Baba*. How are you? You know, what happened in the end?'

His father beamed from ear to ear and attempted to sit up before settling back grimacing slightly, 'I know, I watched the game. You took a beating.'

Arjun shrugged, 'It was nothing'.

His father went on, 'I know, and I am so proud of you. Now you see, believing in yourself, no matter what the odds are, is paramount. Even more important than the eventual result.'

Arjun looked at his father seriously, 'I batted with your gloves, you know.'

'And you did them proud. What's next?' his father asked.

'I am going back to my books. Cricket is all right and I want it to be my career, but I must have a back up plan. I may even consider becoming a doctor,' Arjun asserted with a twinkle on his eyes. 'Cricket may just be a pleasurable pastime.'

His father laughed, 'I am glad you have thought of a plan 'B'. Particularly, the way you played at the end of the innings. You just might need another career.'

He suddenly clutched his chest, Arjun started up worriedly.

His father settled back and continued, 'It feels good to laugh. Hurts, but feels good.'

Arjun touched the stitches on his face and winced, 'Hurts, but feels good,' he echoed.

The next morning Arjun walked out from his building, Pranay, Rahim and other kids were in the midst of a keenly fought game of cricket. Rahim broke away and walked over to him.

'Here comes the high and mighty test cricketer. He is a big shot now, won't play with us!'

Arjun smiled and started walking away. He wanted to get to the hospital early; his father was coming home. Rahim continued. 'Or are you just scared. Give me three balls and I'll get you.'

Arjun hesitated and then gestured for the bat. Rahim walked back to his extra long run up and sent in two sizzling fast deliveries that Arjun patted back demurely. Rahim was thinking. There was almost an audible creak. With the body language of a man with a plan he trundled up a few steps and delivered the last ball 'left arm slow' round the wicket. Arjun rocked back and pulled the ball just as Pallavi screamed, 'No!' The ball soared in a perfect parabola and found the center of the sole surviving pane in Mrs. Gadkari's window. The resounding crash was followed by silence. Momentary silence. Momentary, before Mrs. Gadkari's shrill voice filled the airwaves,

'*Melyano! Kartyano!*' Couldn't hit like that in Pakistan......!'

Arjun closed his eyes. The picture was still clear.

THE END